"Do you bring all your conquests here?"

"Actually, you're the first," Lucas told her, his mood as dark as the swamp below.

And that's when Willa knew she was treading on very dangerous ground. Lorna had warned her about Lucas's lighthearted nature. But her friend had failed to warn her about the other qualities that made up Lucas Dorsette. He was obviously an interesting man. A man who had a deeper, more spiritual side that he hid from the world.

"Thank you for showing me this place, Lucas."

"Thank you for letting me bring you here," he replied, his tone neither carefree nor careless.

Which made her wonder all over again.

Books by Lenora Worth

Love Inspired

LENORA WORTH

grew up in a small Georgia town and decided in the fourth grade that she wanted to be a writer. But first she married her high school sweetheart, then moved to Atlanta, Georgia. Taking care of their baby daughter at home while her husband worked at night, Lenora discovered the world of romance novels and knew that's what she wanted to write. And so she began.

A few years later the family settled in Shreveport, Louisiana, where Lenora continued to write while working as a marketing assistant. After the birth of her second child, a boy, she decided to pursue her dream full-time. In 1993 Lenora's hard work and determination finally paid off with that first sale.

"I never gave up, and I believe my faith in God helped get me through the rough times when I doubted myself," Lenora says. "Each time I start a new book, I say a prayer, asking God to give me the strength and direction to put the words to paper. That's why I'm so thrilled to be a part of Steeple Hill's Love Inspired line, where I can combine my faith in God with my love of romance. It's the best combination."

Something Beautiful
Lenora Worth

Love Inspired®

Published by Steeple Hill Books™

STEEPLE HILL BOOKS

Steeple
Hill™

ISBN 0-373-87176-7

SOMETHING BEAUTIFUL

Copyright © 2002 by Lenora H. Nazworth

This edition published by arrangement with Steeple Hill Books.

® and TM are trademarks of Steeple Hill Books, used under license. Trademarks indicated with ® are registered in the United States Patent and Trademark Office, the Canadian Trade Marks Office and in other countries.

Visit us at www.steeplehill.com

Printed in U.S.A.

So we do not lose heart....
For this slight momentary affliction
is preparing us for an eternal weight of glory
beyond all measure, because we look at what
cannot be seen; for what can be seen is temporary,
but what cannot be seen is eternal.

—2 Corinthians 4:16-18

In memory of my mother-in-law, Patsy.
And to all the breast cancer survivors out there.

Chapter One

She was a vision in the mist.

Lucas Dorsette quietly eased his pirogue through the dark, brackish swamp waters, maneuvering the long paddle pole around blue-blossomed water hyacinths and gnarled gray cypress stumps until he reached the boathouse nestled between the back garden and the bayou. But he stopped before anchoring the small canoelike boat against the weathered dock.

He looked again through the low mist, just to make sure he wasn't imagining the woman who stood under the ancient weeping willow tree on the shore, her head turned so he could see her profile as she looked over the dark, chocolate waters of the bayou.

No, he wasn't seeing things. This vision was real.

And she was exactly his type.

She was tall and slender, with a classic face that spoke of strong bone structure. She held her arms wrapped against her midsection, as if to ward off the humid chill the rising dawn had left. Long blond hair that changed from white-gold to rich yellow in the growing light hung down her back almost to her waist. She was wearing white—a long, flowing cotton dress that made Lucas think of other, more simple times. The woman looked as if she'd just stepped out of another century.

Curious, Lucas kept his eyes on her while he roped the pirogue to the dock. Then he hopped on the planked boards, his actions quick and quiet, so as not to startle the woman who stood only a few feet away, her eyes centered on the water, her body turned away from the summer gardens of Bayou le Jardin.

Lucas stood there in amazement, his gaze taking in the woman with the old southern mansion behind her. He had to swallow, blink his eyes. It was the way the rays of first light shot down from the sky to touch the woman's face there in the soft mist, as if the very hand of God was reaching out to this fascinating stranger.

Which certainly made for a breathtaking picture. One Lucas would surely never forget.

In her long white dress with the early morning breeze lifting her thick, lush hair from her shoulders, she looked as if she belonged right there in that spot under the willow tree. Especially with the backdrop of his beloved home behind her.

The stark, classic beauty of the mansion always left Lucas a bit awestruck, even though he'd lived here since he was nine years old. He respected the quiet dignity of the old house, though he rarely stayed in his bedroom on the third floor.

Lucas preferred the swamp to the house, preferred

the gardens to the parlor, preferred to be left to his own devices whenever time and duty permitted. He had a nice, cozy cabin deep in the swamp, a cabin he'd salvaged and renovated with his own hands, along with the help of some good, hardworking people. He had ample food from the gardens, the fields and the bayou; he had good books to read at night and good tunes to play on his saxophone when the mood struck him. He had his plane to fly when he wanted to be up above it all, his horse to ride when he wanted to feel the wind on his face, and he had several lucrative ventures going, enough to bring in plenty of cash for a man of simple means. And he had friends to find on a lonely Saturday night and church to attend on any given Sunday. Aunt Hilda would remind him that he had the blessed assurance of Jesus Christ, too, of course. If he ever stood still long enough to listen for it.

Lucas was content to travel through the bayou, content to watch over his aunt Hilda and his sisters, Lorna and Lacey. Content to flirt shamelessly with all the local belles while never seriously getting involved with any of them. He'd never wanted for anything else.

Until now.

Now, Lucas saw the home he loved, the home he respected and had vowed to watch over, in a different light.

Now he saw *her* there in the picture—this mysterious, lovely creature who'd somehow appeared, like a vibrant flower sprung to life, in the dew-kissed gardens.

Lucas didn't know who the woman was.

But he certainly intended to find out.

His sisters accused him of falling in love too easily and too often, and he supposed that was right.

'Cause it was about to happen again. In a very big way.

Lucas grinned, then started walking toward the woman, instinct telling him this time things might be different. Because this time, he knew in his heart he'd just stumbled across…something beautiful.

And then the cameras started flashing.

Lucas blinked twice, watched as the tranquil woman whirled and with a loud groan took off in a mad dash toward the house, her long hair and long dress flying around her as if she were a runaway bride.

The cameras followed her. Two of them with big zoom lenses, carried by two rather burly-looking men who'd popped out from behind a cluster of camellia bushes.

"Willa?" one of the men shouted. "Just one picture, Willa. C'mon, people want to know why you backed out of that runway show in New York!"

"Go away," the woman shouted in a voice that was as cultured and gleaming as the single strand of pearls she wore around her neck. "I don't have anything to say to you."

But the two determined photographers kept right on coming. Like a set of hound dogs chasing a rabbit into the swamp, they practically fell over each other in their haste to get to the elusive woman.

Lucas watched, angered and amazed, as one of the

overstuffed men stomped right through Aunt Hilda's prized miniature rose garden then almost tripped over his own feet as he sprinted to get a close-up of the woman he'd called Willa.

"Get away from me," the woman said, her hands on her hips, her stare full of anger and defiance.

The cameras took it all in, clicking with a constant whine. One of the men laughed. "Good shot. That'll make the cover."

"I'll get a better one for *my* cover," the other one snarled.

Lucas took two long strides and stepped between the beauty and the beasts.

"You heard the woman," he said on a low growl, one hand shoving at the first man while he held his other hand in warning toward the second photographer. "Get away from her now."

"And who are you?" Burly Number One asked, his double chin jutting over his cheap navy and red striped tie.

Lucas grinned, then shifted his gaze from one man to the other. Slapping a hand across the rough denim of his jeans, he turned and winked at the beauty who'd automatically taken up a position behind his protective back. "Who am I? *Moi?*" He chuckled low, then shook his head. "I'll tell you who I am. I'm Lucas Dorsette. I live here. And you two seem to be pestering this lovely lady, not to mention trespassing on private property."

Burly Number Two looked at Number One, rolled his eyes, then adjusted his heavy camera. "Let's go, man."

"We weren't talking to *him*," Number One replied, frowning at Lucas. "And *I* just wanted a minute with *you*, Willa. Just a couple of pictures for this week's issue."

"Me, too," Number Two added, glaring at the other photographer. "We have a much bigger circulation than that rag *he* works for."

Lucas turned to smile at the woman and felt the up-close essence of her beauty in a gut punch right to his stomach. It was hard to speak, but he managed to keep his cool so he could continue defending that beauty and look good in her eyes. "Willa, do you have anything to say to these two…gentlemen?"

"Not a word," she replied, gratitude sparkling like rainwater in her breathtaking crystal-blue gaze. "I'd really like them to just go away," she added through a perfect row of clenched gleaming white teeth.

Lucas shrugged, then dropped his hands to his sides. "Then I guess that settles it, *hein?*" Taking a step toward the two photographers, he said, "Get off my property right now or I will call the sheriff."

"Let's go," Number Two told Number One, backing away. "We got enough pictures, anyway."

"Speak for yourself," Number One retorted, posing his camera toward Willa. Until he saw the look in Lucas's eyes. Then he shrugged and brushed past the apparent competition. "Okay, guess I do need to get back to my hotel room and get these developed— so I can beat *you* to the scoop."

The race was on as the two jostled each other.

"Hey, hold on there, fellows," Lucas said, surprising the entire group. Then he turned to the woman. "Do you want these two to have pictures of you?"

"No," she said, her incredible eyes burning holes through the two motley, perspiring men.

Lucas held his hand up, motioning to the two. "Let's have it, please."

"Have what?" It was a whining chorus.

"The film," Lucas replied, a smile forming on his lips. "Now."

"You can't take our film," Burly Number One protested, sweat popping on his pale forehead.

"Watch me, *mon ami*." Lucas grabbed the man's camera, opened it and took the film out, inch by inch.

"Hey, you just ruined that!"

"Yes, I did." Then he turned to the other man, his hand outstretched. "Hand it over, unless you want me to report you to the authorities."

Reluctantly, and with great disgust, the man handed over the roll of film from his camera. "That belongs to me, you know. To *Famous Faces* magazine."

"Yeah, well, now it belongs to me," Lucas stated as he dropped the ruined film on the ground and rubbed his suede hiking boot across it, disdain evident in his actions. "Now, leave the way you came in—which was probably over the side fence." He'd have to remember to have Tobbie check that broken fence again.

"Can't you let us out the gate?" Number One whined.

Lucas turned his head in a gesture of disbelief. "Since I didn't invite you in, why should I be gracious in letting you out?'' Then he motioned toward the driveway that wound around the gardens. ''Dig a trench, for all I care, but get out of here, and don't let me catch you back again. Ever. Or mine will be the only famous face you remember.''

''You'll be hearing from my publisher,'' one of the men called as they trudged away, both huffing and puffing.

''I'll look forward to it,'' Lucas replied, chuckling. He pulled a walkie-talkie off his leather belt.

''Tobbie, you there?'' At Tobbie's crisp answer, Lucas said, ''Two men are approaching the side fence, that place near the tulip gardens where the fence needs repairing. Would you kindly escort them off the property?''

''With pleasure, for true,'' Tobbie said, his hoot of laughter echoing over the static.

Satisfied that the oversize Tobbie Babineaux would scare the living daylights out of the two and send them packing, Lucas grinned.

And then her turned to *her.* ''Fans of yours?''

Willa O'Connor looked at the man who'd come to her rescue and wished she knew how to answer his question.

''Not exactly,'' she replied, still in shock after being ambushed in what she'd taken to be an isolated, secluded spot. ''They work for some of those supermarket tabloids. *Celebrity Exposé* and, as you heard, *Famous Faces.* They like to travel in packs so they can attack from several different angles, then fight each other for the best shots.''

''So you're a celebrity, then?''

"Somewhat," she replied, not wanting to reveal too much.

She waited as the man took his time letting that little tidbit settle in. While he did that, he looked her over, his dark eyes full of doubt and mirth, his olive skin alive with a fine sheen of sweat in spite of the early morning breezes. He was certainly a handsome thing, with his long, curling brown-black hair and those chocolate-colored eyes that seemed to take in everything around him with a careless, lazy observation.

"Lucas," she said, recognition making her gasp as she remembered the name he'd given the two reporters. "You're Lorna's brother, right?"

"*Oui,* and her favorite brother, at that," he said, his grin full of promise and trouble as he reached a hand toward hers. "And from what I gathered from those two camera-toting clowns, your name is Willa?"

Willa tentatively took his hand, shaking it as she nodded then tried to pull away. But he held her. His hand was warm and work-callused, with long, artistic fingers that seemed to cling to her palm a bit too much for comfort. Lucas Dorsette didn't just shake her hand; he held it as if it were a treasure. And then he did something even more unexpected. He bent his head and kissed her hand.

"Hello, Willa," he said as he lifted his head, those dark, mischievous eyes sparkling with way too much charm. "Where on earth did you come from?"

"She came from New York," Lorna said from

behind him. "And she'd probably like her hand back, big brother."

Willa watched as Lucas shrugged, then turned his head toward his sister and her husband, Mick, as they strolled down the garden path from the house. But he didn't let go of her hand. Instead, he kept it tucked in his then brought it down, holding it as if they'd been lifelong friends. "I'll give it back…in a little bit."

Willa didn't wait for him to decide when. She gave him a slight smile, then pulled her hand away so she could wave to Lorna, glad for the distraction and glad to have her tingling hand away from his overly warm fingers. "Hello there. I was just about to explain to your brother what I'm doing here."

"Let me," Lorna said, giving Willa a light hug. Then she turned to Lucas. "Lucas, this is my friend Willa O'Connor. She arrived late last night. I met Willa in Paris a few years ago, and we've kept in touch since then. She needed a few days to herself, so I invited her to come down here to Bayou le Jardin. And I expect you to give her some much-needed space." Then she yanked playfully on a silky strand of her brother's unkempt hair. "*And* I expect you to behave yourself."

"Don't I always now?" Lucas said, his gaze zooming in on Willa with all the bright-eyed intent of someone who never, ever behaved himself.

Oh, she loved his accent—part southern gentleman, part backwoods Cajun, slow and easy and downright irresistible. Lucas Dorsette was everything his sister had described and more. A true contradiction—fierce and gentle, mysterious and gallant. Handsome and fun-loving.

A lethal combination of charm and rebellion.

Lorna *had* warned her.

But he had come to her rescue like some gallant knight from a romance novel. Only who was she kidding? Willa knew she needed another man in her life like she needed another pair of designer shoes. She'd had way too many of both.

And she'd come down to Louisiana to clean her closet, get the cobwebs out of the attic, so to speak. Decide what to do about her crumbling life. She didn't need Lorna's handsome brother complicating her already complicated existence.

And yet, she could still feel the warmth of his lips on the back of her hand.

"Your brother has behaved perfectly this morning," she told Lorna. "He helped me out of a very sticky situation."

"What happened?" Lorna asked as she leaned against her good-looking husband's chest. Mick automatically wrapped his arms around Lorna, holding her close as they waited for Willa to answer.

Willa envied the happiness her friend had found in the spring, envied Lorna's glowing face and contented newlywed smile. She was glad Lorna had found some peace at last. She'd come to Lorna's beloved gardens hoping to find some peace of her own.

But apparently, it wasn't to be.

"I'm afraid I've been found," she said. "The press—two goons from the tabloids."

"They were hiding in the bushes like possums,"

Lucas said, his dark brows lifting as he watched Willa. "And hey, *jolie fille,* mind telling me what that was all about? Why did those two want pictures of you so bad, besides the fact that you're beautiful and so obviously photogenic, and as you said, somewhat of a celebrity?"

Willa had to smile at the innocence of his question. A man who didn't know her face? A man who really didn't follow every aspect of her career? She found that hard to believe, but it was a refreshing change, at least.

Lorna gave her brother a gentle slap on the arm. "You dolt, don't you *know* who she is?"

Lucas nodded. "Yes, she's Willa O'Connor, fair maiden and friend of Lorna. Isn't that all I need to know?"

"Yes," Willa said.

"No," Lorna replied, rolling her eyes. Then she took her brother by the face, holding a hand to his jaw. "Willa is a supermodel. Her face is famous all over the world. And right now, she's supposed to be resting—away from all the cameras and the spotlights. So you did the right thing by sending those two away."

"They'll be back, and they'll bring others with them," Willa stated, her head down. "Which means I probably should leave soon. I don't want to disrupt your home or bother any of your other guests."

"Nonsense," Lucas said before Lorna could reply, his dark eyes gleaming with new knowledge. "If you came here to find rest and relaxation, then that's exactly what you'll get. And I'll put myself personally in charge—just to make sure.''

Lorna's husband, Mick, spoke up. ''How, uh, noble of you, Lucas.''

''Ain't it, though?'' Lucas replied, clearly unaffected by his brother-in-law's teasing. ''Personal detail—I'm good at that. I can be your tour guide, your bodyguard, whatever you need me to be.'' He held his hand over his heart, then gave Willa a besotted, lopsided grin that had her laughing in spite of herself.

But the way he'd spoken left her wondering exactly what his many talents entailed. Probably heartbreaker, rake, charmer, just to name a few.

''Easy, brother,'' Lorna cautioned. ''She needs to rest. And if I know you, that word translates more into restless. Don't drag her out into the swamp for any 'gator sightings just yet.''

Lucas looked affronted. ''The swamp can be a very restful spot. And highly romantic.''

Willa had to smile again. ''Rest I need. And as for romance, I'm afraid I've given up on that forever.''

''Forever is a long time, suga','' Lucas countered. ''Me, personally, I couldn't survive without a little romance now and then.''

His dark, unwavering gaze washed over her, telling her that neither could she—if he had his way.

''I warned you,'' Lorna reminded Willa, taking her husband's hand to head to the house. ''Breakfast is ready, if you can tear yourself away from my poetic brother.''

''I'll escort you,'' Lucas told Willa, tucking his arm around hers before she could take a step. ''According to our aunt Hilda, breakfast is the most important meal of the day.''

"Willa's already met Aunt Hilda," Lorna called over her shoulder. "She had an early meeting in town so she couldn't stay for breakfast with our guests, but she did urge Willa to eat a good meal."

"See?" Lucas ducked his head low, his words coming in a warm rush near Willa's ear. "And she always let's me say grace."

Grace. Willa wondered what that word meant, exactly. She'd been told she had a natural grace. She was in demand because of that, at the top of her career. And she'd just walked out on one of the most important fashion shows in the industry. How was that for having grace? How was that for saving grace?

She knew Lorna's family was devout. Lorna had never made any secret of her Christianity, nor of her strong faith. Was that what real grace was all about? And could this beautiful, timeless garden really bring Willa the spiritual and physical healing her doctor and her friend had told her she needed?

Not if her first morning here was any indication. Two photographers in the bushes and a handsome Cajun on her arm, and all before breakfast.

"I've been up since before dawn. I'm stark, raving starving, and beating off thugs only added to my appetite," Lucas said, bringing her out of her tormented, confused thoughts.

Willa had to wonder how he stayed in such good shape if he ate like a madman all the time. But she decided it'd be better to put such thoughts out of her

mind. "Thanks for your help back there," she told
him, meaning it. "I was hoping no one would find
me here."

"They won't again—not with me on the case, I
guarantee."

He'd stretched out that last word, his Cajun accent
every bit as teasing as his merry grin. Obviously, he
wasn't as concerned about intrusive reporters as she
was.

"I don't expect you to be my protector, Lucas. I'm
capable of handling them myself. After all, I'm used
to it."

He looked at her, those dark, dancing eyes touching her as closely as his arm holding hers. And making her feel extremely warm in the morning sunshine.
"So you're a model. That figures. You've got the
face and figure for it."

Willa looked away, toward the house where the
few other guests had gathered around the long buffet
table set on the downstairs gallery. "That's what they
tell me. Always in demand."

If Lucas noticed the sarcasm in her tone, he didn't
let on. "But you didn't come down here to be in
demand, so you don't have to handle it while you're
here. I'll beef up security and make sure we watch
everyone who comes in and out the gate. If you came
here to rest, then that's what we want you to do."

Rest. The word made Willa want to sit down on
that lovely old swing behind the big house and rock
back and forth all day. Maybe with Lucas there to
tease her and make her smile. Quickly shaking off
that particular image, she told him, "This is certainly

a perfect spot for rest and relaxation. I don't know why I waited so long to accept Lorna's invitation.''

Lucas pulled her close, his dark head almost touching hers as he whispered in her ear. ''I sure wish you'd come sooner, and that's a fact. We're still recovering from the spring floods, but the gardens are coming along fine.''

The warmth of him was just too much. Willa managed to extract herself from him as they reached the back gallery, where Lorna had a full breakfast set up on the wrought-iron buffet table. ''Well, I have a fact for you,'' she told Lucas as she pretended to be interested in the food. ''I need coffee.''

''That we've got. Hot and strong.''

''Then I'll be perfectly content.''

''What about all this food? I reckon even supermodels need to eat,'' he said, his arm somehow linked once again through hers. ''Aren't you hungry?''

His closeness seemed like a natural thing. Lucas was probably used to touching, hugging, being close to people.

She wasn't.

''Maybe a little,'' she replied, feeling sick to her stomach as she scanned the fresh banana bread and strawberry muffins, grits, eggs, bacon and fruit the other guests seemed to be devouring.

Lucas shoved a gleaming white plate at her. ''Well, Lorna's probably made a big production— brunch with an old friend and all. You'll find we love to eat around here.''

Willa swallowed, thinking she probably wouldn't

be able to eat a bite. After her encounter with those photographers, she was too keyed up, too worried, too nervous to eat. She had a lot of things to work through in her time here. A lot of decisions to make. She couldn't let Lucas Dorsette's charming, easy ways sidetrack her. Even if he did smell so good—like water and trees, like fresh air after a slow, soft country rain.

Once again, Willa reminded herself she'd better keep such thoughts out of her head. Way too dangerous.

But she certainly could allow Lucas to show her around a little bit, act as swamp guide, maybe. That couldn't hurt.

Unless he kept looking at her the way he was looking at her right now.

Willa couldn't allow Lucas to get too close.

Because she knew in her heart that would be the worst thing that could happen. For both of them.

Chapter Two

"Do you have any of those fashion magazines lying around?" Lucas asked Lacey when they were alone in the kitchen.

He'd excused himself from Willa and Lorna so he could follow Lacey inside. He wanted to see for himself that Willa O'Connor was truly a fashion model. Not that he doubted it. She was the perfect example of high fashion. He wanted to be able to stare at her without anyone noticing, and he figured finding a glossy picture of her in a magazine would do the trick until he could figure out how to be around her twenty-four hours a day and still get his work done.

Lacey shot her brother a quizzical look, then grinned. "I see you've met Willa."

Lucas nodded, grabbed a fresh sweet-potato roll, then chewed thoughtfully before answering. "I didn't just meet her. I saw her standing in the morning mist on the banks of the bayou and lost my heart to her forever."

Lacey nodded, then went right on placing fresh fruit on a tray for the breakfast guests gathered on the back gallery. "Uh-huh. How many times have I heard you say something such as that, only to find some poor brokenhearted woman at church the next Sunday, glaring at you across the pew because you suddenly found you wanted to keep your fickle heart intact, after all?"

"Ouch, that hurts. You're cruel, Lacey, love. Very cruel."

"And you wouldn't know real love if it bit you on your adorable nose," his older sister countered as she headed out the open French doors. Then she turned to face him, all seriousness and as prim and proper as ever in her pearls and lace. "Lucas, be careful with this one, will you please? From what Lorna's told me, Willa O'Connor is dealing with some major issues right now. She doesn't need you pestering her with one of your obsessive but rather short-lived infatuations."

Lucas didn't answer her. He stood, leaning against the counter, his eyes scanning the small crowd to make sure the object of this discussion was still chatting with Lorna and Mick. And wondered what issues lay behind Willa's incredible blue-eyed million-dollar smile.

But Lacey wasn't finished. "Besides, I don't think Willa is the type to fall for your irresistible charms. She's way too smart for the likes of you. She went to school at some fancy college up north, graduated with honors."

Leave it to Lacey to drop a zinger like that with

a sweet, serene smile plastered across her classic face. Lucas let out an aggravated sigh as he watched his sister play hostess with all the ingrained manners of a true Southern lady. And wished he could do something really childish like put a lizard down her starched collar.

"Do *you* have a magazine?" he asked Rosie Lee Babineaux, their longtime housekeeper and cook, as she passed him on her way to the industrial-size refrigerator.

"Lucas, Lucas," Rosie Lee replied, laughing so hard her shoulders shook. "You need to put your eyeballs back in your head, *hein?*"

"Am I that obvious?"

"You got the look," Rosie Lee told him, wagging a finger at him, her Cajun accent twice as distinctive as his.

"And what look would that be, *chère?*"

"That Lucas look," Rosie Lee explained, rolling her eyes. "The one you get whenever a pretty woman is anywhere within five miles of you."

Lucas knew she was right. But, hey, he was having fun with it, so why couldn't everyone lay off? "I just want to investigate things a bit further," he explained. "Maybe hang a picture of her near my pillow, so I can gaze at her with adoration...."

Rosie Lee's burst of laughter stopped him. She had to wipe her eyes, but she lifted a hand toward a set of swinging doors. "I think Em left a few fancy magazines in our sitting room. Go see."

Lucas took off like a rocket, heading into the small family room tucked off the kitchen, a place where he'd spent many happy hours with the Babineaux clan since he'd arrived, nine years old and scared to death, at Bayou le Jardin. Falling across a worn plaid couch that had been salvaged and cleaned since the spring floods, he remembered feeling safe here in this little room that had at one time been servants' quarters. He'd naturally blended right in with the six Babineaux children. To the point that they'd included him as one of their own—just like another son, even though he was a few years older than their four boys and two girls.

Glancing around, Lucas remembered Tobias Babineaux, or Big Tobbie, as everyone called him, teaching him all about the dark, mysterious swamp waters that ran behind the grounds of Bayou le Jardin. Tobbie had taken Lucas under his wing, teaching him how to hunt and fish and track, teaching him how to show respect to Mother Nature and how to stand up for what he believed in, teaching him how to survive.

And Lucas had drunk it all in, wanting very much to survive, but always, always challenging life in the midst of learning his lessons well.

A daredevil. That's what they'd called him.

Reckless. Juvenile. Too full of life for his own good. That's what he'd always heard about himself.

Too full of life. So full of life that he dared anyone or anything to change that fact.

Even God.

And because of that reckless, careless streak, Lucas had come close, so close to getting into serious trouble over the years, that he'd reached the point where everyone just left him to it—as if they'd all given up on changing him.

But that didn't stop his loving sisters from reminding him on a daily basis of his shortcomings.

"Why start worrying about that now?" he said with a shrug as he looked around for the much-coveted magazine. Right now, he wouldn't dwell on how lousy he'd felt since the spring night all those months ago when he'd left Lorna alone in the mansion, in the dark.

He wouldn't stop to think about what she must have suffered before Mick had found her there. And saved her from herself.

"It should have been me," Lucas said as he reached into a cabinet and grabbed a handful of tattered fashion magazines.

But then again, Lucas knew in his heart it had to be Mick. Mick Love had fallen in love with his sister in spite of her fears and her self-doubts. And Lucas had accepted that, welcomed it. It was only fitting that Mick be the one to come to Lorna's aid, to bring her such strength in her faith and herself again. But still...Lucas couldn't get past that night.

And the promise he had made to his sisters so long ago, on another dark, storm-tossed night.

"Did you find it?"

Lucas looked up to see Rosie Lee's round, olive-skinned face smiling at him, her long black, silver-streaked braid swinging over one shoulder. "Did you find what you were looking for?" she asked, a teasing light in her dark eyes.

"I hope so," Lucas said, winking at her as he

made a point of lazily flipping through the pages of a thick magazine. Then more to himself than her, he repeated his wish. "I certainly hope so."

"So, now you've heard all the news about us," Lorna said to Willa. "It's your turn."

Willa sank back against the soft floral cushions of her chair, a fork in one hand while she pretended to eat more breakfast. True, she had managed to down some fresh strawberries and cantaloupe and a freshly baked, grain-rich roll. But she couldn't force herself to eat anything more, in spite of her friend's best efforts.

Hoping to keep the focus of the conversation off herself, Willa glanced across the table at Lorna and Mick. "Even though I missed your wedding because of that shoot in Spain, I'm so happy for both of you. Surviving a tornado and then a flood, only to find each other…that's a remarkable story."

Lorna looked at her husband. "Yes, very remarkable, considering how I resisted Mick from the first day."

"But it was love at first sight for me, I think," Mick replied, his hand reaching for his wife. "We've been through a lot together, that's for sure. My whole life changed once I set foot on this old plantation."

Willa was amazed that Mick Love had been willing to pick up and move to be with the woman he loved. She'd never known a man with that type of commitment, a man willing to give up everything, change his whole lifestyle because of being in love. Her mother had done that all these years, followed the man she loved, but Willa had to wonder, if it were the other way around, would her father have done the same? She doubted it, so she had to question Mick further. "And you didn't mind—moving here, relocating your business?"

"Why should I?" Mick said, his hand trailing through Lorna's hair. "I didn't really have anything to lose. Business is better than ever, I've got a wonderful wife to come home to each night, and hey, my best friend even relocated here with me and married the woman of his dreams, too. He's training to be a fireman."

"It must be the coffee," Willa said, laughing. Maybe that would explain why she kept looking for Lucas to come to the table. He'd hopped up a few minutes ago, excused himself with a flourish, then disappeared inside the kitchen. And why did she care?

"There is something about Bayou le Jardin," Mick agreed, finishing his brew. "It...can heal all wounds."

Lorna nodded. "Aunt Hilda—you met her earlier, before she headed off to work—firmly believes that we are all closer to Christ here in this garden. She takes her troubles to Him and she's taught us to do the same."

Mick shrugged. "But it took a tornado and a flood for me to understand that concept."

"You really believe that?" Willa asked, wishing with all her heart that Mick was right. She needed to be healed, both physically and spiritually. "That God somehow had a hand in bringing you here?"

Mick got up, looked at Lorna, then nodded. "Oh, yeah. I'm a believer now." With that, he kissed his wife. "And...I've gotta get to work. Justin needs some help with a little pruning, then I have to ride into Kenner to do an estimate on that remodeling work we've been discussing." He lifted a hand. "We're still trying to get this place back the way it was before the storms. And that is going to take some doing, considering we still have some water damage." He touched Lorna's hair again. "I probably won't be back in my office in town for a few hours, so I'll see you later this afternoon, okay?"

"Okay," Lorna replied, her gaze filled with love as she kissed her husband. "Don't work too hard."

Mick grinned, then waved to Willa. "Hope you enjoy your stay."

"Thank you," Willa told him. After he left, she sighed long and hard. "Lorna, he's..."

"Perfect?" Lorna asked, her expression dreamy and serene. "Mick has helped me in more ways than I ever dreamed possible. He's brought me peace, made me feel secure, helped me get over my fear of the dark. He still has to travel a good bit, but I'm okay with that—it's part of his job. And sometimes I take off and head out with him."

"I'm so glad," Willa told her, meaning it. "I envy you."

"Don't," Lorna replied, concern bringing a frown to her face. "You can find happiness, too, Willa. I know it. I believe that now—I didn't believe in happily ever after before."

"But you're in love, married to the perfect man. That tends to change one's perspective on these things."

"Actually, Mick is far from perfect, but he's a good, decent man and…just like Mick, I truly believe God brought us together here in this old garden."

Willa was much too cynical and jaded to believe that. She'd seen too many broken relationships, been a part of too many herself, to ever believe there was such a thing as a lifetime love between two destined people. Fate was way too fickle for that to happen.

Then she looked up to find Lucas Dorsette leaning against a rounded white column, his eyes centered on her, his expression a mixture of curious charm and conquering hero. He gave her a soul-searing smile, then lowered his head, appearing to be completely engrossed in a magazine.

"What's the story with your adorable brother?" she asked Lorna. "Does he break hearts by the week, or only on a monthly installment?"

Lorna shot her hovering brother a long look. "Oh, Lucas breaks hearts on a daily basis. I think every single woman at church has tried to win him over to matrimony, but our Lucas is a sly one. He can see them coming a mile away, so he flirts with them, teases them, makes them think they are the only one, and then he moves on. He treats women like flowers, picking them and enjoying them until they wilt away, then he discards them for another fresh bloom."

Willa studied Lucas, glad she was immune to charming, shallow men, but somehow disappointed to hear that Lucas might be that way. "You certainly don't paint him in a very pretty light."

"Just being honest with you," Lorna replied. "Lucas is a wonderful person, the best brother in the world, and I love him dearly. But…he doesn't take life very seriously."

"Maybe we could all learn a lesson from that," Willa replied, thinking she took everything far too seriously for her own good. Which was why she was in such turmoil right now.

Lorna nodded. "As long as you remember, with Lucas, it's all a big game. Enjoy it while you're here, Willa, but just be forewarned. My brother will never settle down."

Willa groaned, then shrugged. "I'm not looking to settle down. You of all people should know I'm not here looking for love, and I certainly have no intention of trying to snare your elusive brother."

Lorna reached out a hand to her. "I know. You need to find some peace and quiet, and you really need to rest…and take care of yourself. We can't forget your reasons for coming here. I just don't want my beautiful brother interfering with that process."

"Why can't I be part of the process?" Lucas said from behind them, making both of them jump.

Willa sat bolt upright. She'd only looked away for a minute. How had he moved so quickly and so quietly?

Another thing to remember about Lucas Dorsette, she supposed.

Lorna didn't bat an eye as she got up. "You can

be a lot of things while Willa is here," she told her
brother. "A companion, a tour guide, a security
guard. But Willa needs to—"

"I know, I know," he interrupted, holding up a
hand. "Willa needs her rest. Willa needs to be left
alone. Willa needs to know that Lucas is walking
trouble and not worth a minute of her time. Did I
leave anything out?"

Lorna reached out a hand to touch his face. "That
just about covers it." Then she kissed him on the
cheek. "I know I can trust you, so be nice."

Lucas grabbed his sister's hand, his gaze changing
with mercurial speed from teasing to intense. "Do
you know that, really? Can I be trusted?"

Lorna tightened her hand in his. "Yes, you can.
I've always trusted you, Lucas. And I know what
you're thinking. But...I'm fine. I'm great. Mick is
taking good care of me, and we're very happy. So
stop worrying."

Confused by the exchange, Willa felt uncomfortable. As if she'd stepped into an intimate setting
where she didn't belong. But then, she'd never been
so close to another person that she could share a sort
of language, the way Lorna and Lucas seemed to talk
to each other. Almost in riddles, but they both
seemed to understand each other exactly.

She'd noticed that about them, and Lacey, too. She
knew they'd survived a terrible horror only to grow
up secure in their faith and to become closer as a
family. Sharing that kind of bond had held them together, but as Lorna had told her months ago when

she'd called Willa to invite her to the wedding, perhaps that bond had also held them captive.

And yet, Willa wished she'd had some sort of bond to make her closer to her parents. They'd never really been a family, the three of them. They'd co-existed in a big, rambling house. That is, whenever they were there together.

Family. The word always made Willa flinch. Oh, she had a family. A mother and father who adored her but who also wanted to control her. But she'd never really felt loved, for some strange reason. Not in the way Lorna seemed loved, at least.

She envied her friend. And longed to get to know the intriguing Lucas Dorsette.

"Me, worry?" Lucas shrugged and lifted his dark brows, bringing Willa's thoughts to the present. "Never."

"I have to get to the restaurant and start things for the lunch crowd," Lorna said to Willa. "Will you be okay?"

"I think I'm going to wander around in the gardens," Willa told her, intensely aware that Lucas was watching her. "Maybe finally read that thick romance novel I've been carting around for months now."

"We're still recovering from the flood," Lucas said, his hand lifting in an arc. "But I'd be happy to show you some of the more beautiful spots."

"That sounds nice." She glanced at Lorna, saw no censure in her friend's eyes and breathed a sigh of relief.

She'd been warned about Lucas Dorsette too many times to care. She didn't understand why his sisters seemed so concerned that he'd break her heart. She'd turned down suitors from all over the world, after all. Playboys, a prince or two, politicians, they'd all courted her and some had tried to corrupt her. But luckily, the one thing her distant, worldly parents had instilled in her was a sense of caution and integrity—an O'Connor could never bring shame or scandal to the family honor. It simply wasn't permitted.

And because Ambassador Eugene O'Connor and his lovely wife, Candace, had frowned on their daughter's choice of careers, Willa had at least tried to stay out of trouble and stay away from the many temptations lurking in the world of high fashion.

Would her parents approve of Lucas Dorsette? Hardly. But she was only going to be here for a short time, and her parents were far away, traveling yet again. Willa was an adult, after all. She could take care of herself; she'd been doing it for most of her life. So she wasn't afraid of spending a few mindless days with Lucas Dorsette.

He seemed harmless enough.

As long as they both kept their perspective, of course. As long as she remembered Lucas liked to keep things light.

Well, so did she.

She wouldn't let the legendary gardens of Bayou le Jardin mess with her head.

And she wouldn't let the legendary Lucas Dorsette mess with her heart.

But when he took her hand and pulled her down a cool, shaded path dripping with ancient hot-pink crape myrtle trees, Willa had a feeling it was already too late to turn back.

Chapter Three

He was taking her off the beaten path.

"Where are we going?" Willa asked Lucas as they moved away from the house and closer to the bayou.

Here the vegetation grew more lush, green and rich, thriving in spite of the summer heat. The smell of wet earth and brackish water mingled with the scent of honeysuckle and wild-blooming jasmine. The mid-morning sun played a game of chance as it tried to pierce the cool shadows cast by the tall, moss-draped cypress trees.

"You'll see," he told her, his hand in hers as he pulled her down the winding path.

"At least it's cooler here."

"One of the many beautiful things about Bayou le Jardin. There's plenty of cool spots, even in the middle of summer. And I happen to know where they all are."

Willa noticed the creepers surrounding the narrowing path—the English ivy that grew wild and free, the ancient camellia bushes and sweet-smelling lilies. She could hear bees buzzing hungrily in the dense garden. She could hear a child's laughter ringing out from the house. Probably that cute little Tobias—the little boy Lucas had rescued during the flood.

Lorna had told her all about that, too. And how Lucas had berated himself for not getting back to the mansion to help Lorna, who had been deathly afraid of the dark, after the electricity had gone off and left Lorna stranded alone in the dark and the flood. Lorna explained that Lucas blamed himself, but no one else saw it that way. He'd saved a child's life. That had to count for something.

She watched his face, wondering what lay behind that square jaw and those lush, full lips. And those dark, mysterious eyes.

The agencies in New York would love a portfolio of pictures of Lucas Dorsette, she figured. His face rivaled those of any of the overpaid male models she knew and worked with on a daily basis. But Lucas had one trait that many of her co-workers didn't possess. He looked completely real, completely male. Not prettied up for the cameras.

And he looked very dangerous.

''I suppose the other guests don't know about this path,'' she said, hoping Lucas would tell her where he was taking her.

She wasn't afraid of being alone with him, but she had this thing about always knowing about what might lie ahead. No surprises. No room for any mistakes.

"*Non.* I keep this one to myself."

"Is it special?"

"I think it is."

So, he was going to be tight-mouthed about this. Willa watched him as he moved in front of her, his feet steady and sure, his steps silent. With his dark good looks and intense concentration, he reminded her of some ancient warrior stalking through a jungle.

Was she his quarry, then?

"Lucas, where are we going?"

He stopped, whirled to stare at her.

His nearness confused her, enticed her, made her want to turn and go back to civilization. Or give up being civilized altogether.

"Are you all right? Tired?"

"I'm fine, just wondering what you're doing."

"I'm taking you to one of my favorite spots."

"Okay."

She decided to stay quiet. He took her hand, guiding her through hanging vines and wild dogwood trees. They moved downward, toward the marsh, then up until they were on a grassy little incline.

"Look," he said, pointing.

Willa followed the direction of his gaze, then laughed. "Oh, my. Well, this was certainly worth the trip."

He'd brought her to a pagoda sitting on top of a moss-covered mound. The pagoda was rustic and ancient, but the wood and stone blending together on the high walls looked solid, and the shingled, slanted roof seemed to be holding up. Or at least, the English ivy was holding the building together. It covered the entire structure and ran down over the mossy rocks that formed the walls of what looked like a walk-through grotto.

A playful morning breeze rustled the nearby tupelo trees, bringing with it the tinkling sound of bells. The almost melancholy melody seemed to be coming from inside the pagoda.

"Chimes," Lucas told her, his keen gaze centering on her face. "I like chimes."

"It's beautiful," she said, her breath coming hard and heavy, whether from the long walk or the sheer beauty of this place, she couldn't say. "So this is your secret garden?"

"You could call it that," Lucas told her as he led her up a narrow stone footpath toward the rectangular structure. "Aunt Hilda discovered it in her younger years, when she could get around more. She showed it to me when I first came here." He smiled, then closed his eyes. "I can still remember what she told me. She said, 'Now, Lucas, most would tell you that this is a temple, a shrine. But we only have one temple—and that is our little chapel where we worship the Lord. This is not a place of worship, but it can be a place of retreat, if you ever need it. God will hear you here in this place, if you need to get away and talk to Him.'"

"She sounds like a fascinating, wise woman."

He opened his eyes, gave Willa one of those heart-stopping looks. "She is. She's traveled all over the world, seen all sorts of shrines and temples, cathedrals and churches, but she loves the Chapel in the

Garden more than anything she's ever seen. And that's where she expects us to be each Sunday.''

Willa thought that was quaint and sweet and again felt that distant tug of longing in her own heart. "And yet, you come here sometimes, to find your peace, talk to God?''

He nodded. ''No one else bothers with this place. Not even Justin, our landscaper. I try to keep the swamp from taking it over completely.''

''So you weed it and clear it out, prune the bramble and sweep away the spiders and snakes?'' She hoped.

He nodded, as silent as the still, waiting wind and trees. Then he said, ''I don't like spiders and snakes, but I respect them. If I find any, I usually send them in the other direction.''

Somewhat comforted, she asked, ''Even the poisonous ones?''

''Even those, unless of course they attack first. Then I don't ask any questions.''

Willa imagined that was probably how he handled life, too. Since he seemed used to being attacked a lot, based on what Lorna had told her.

She could envision him standing here, the hunter in him alert and wary, willing to kill to survive. But she could also see him bending to nudge an innocent creature in the right direction so he wouldn't be forced to harm it. It was that image, rather than the more macho one of him as a hunter and a scrapper, that endeared him to her.

''Well, you've done a good job. It looks well-kept and completely snake free,'' she told him, her gaze taking in the antique sundial centered near the entry-way. "But I have to admit, this place looks a little lost and sad."

"It is," he replied. "It was once a garden spot, centuries ago. It wasn't part of our land then, but the family that owned the neighboring plantation suffered through a yellow fever epidemic, probably brought here from New Orleans. The landowner lost his entire family—his wife, his son and daughter—they all died. He let the place go to ruin during the Civil War, then he died many years later, a lonely, reclusive old man. I'm not sure how my family wound up owning the land—Lacey could tell you all about that—" He stopped, looked at the winding stream that flowed from the Mississippi River to the bayou from the other side of the small, slanting hill. "The story goes that he used to come here and grieve his loss in this hushed, decaying garden. I come here when I'm feeling lost and sad myself. Sometimes I get in that kind of mood. Aunt Hilda says, *c'est l'heure solennelle.*"

"The solemn hour." Willa knew enough French to translate what he'd told her. And wondered why he'd brought her here. Did Lucas sense that she was sad and lost underneath all her fame and fortune?

Just the thought that he might, coupled with the tragic tale he'd told her, brought tears to her eyes. But she quickly dashed them away, not willing to explore the underlying turmoil of her problems right now. She didn't want pity, refused to wallow in self-doubt and despair.

And yet, this place seemed to be beckoning her to

do just that. Or maybe it was telling her to let go and let her inner torment boil to the surface in a cleansing purge. So she could get on with her life. If she had a life to get on with, that is.

Wanting to change her somber thoughts, Willa said, "You don't strike me as the type to wander around moping. From everything Lorna has told me and from what I've seen of you, I wouldn't have imagined you'd have such a place, so beautiful yet so melancholy, tucked away from the world."

He looked at her, his dark eyes locked on hers in a heated black gaze, his secrets as tangled and overgrown as the swamp around them. "'The beauty remains; the pain passes.'"

"What a lovely thing to say."

"You can thank Renoir for that one," he told her, looking away briefly.

"The painter?"

"The very one. He knew a thing or two about pain."

"And it sounds as if you know a thing or two about art," she replied, her opinion of him rapidly changing.

"I know enough to get by. But then, that's how I am about most things in life—whatever it takes to get by." He shifted, ran a hand over his long, curly bangs. "But I didn't bring you here to get you down or talk about art."

She wanted to ask him exactly why he *had* brought her here, but then the smile was back, taking her breath up and away. The tiny bells hanging on a silvery chain just inside the open pagoda door tinkled and laughed along with him, but to Willa, the sound changed in the wind.

It almost sounded like weeping.

"Well, this is a strange and mysterious place," she said, her voice low. "Do you come here a lot?"

"Depends," he said, pulling her into the cool darkness of the rustic structure. "Look over that way." He pointed through one of the open windows toward the path they'd traveled.

Through a gap in the trees and brush, Willa saw the mansion. From this spot atop the small mound, Bayou le Jardin could be seen in all its splendor just to the west. The great evergreen oaks and ever-changing gardens cascaded from the house like colorful lace on a belle's ball gown, while the mansion stood brilliant and sparkling with its Doric columns and classic Greek Revival design.

"How lovely."

"*Oui.* I like to come here and look back at it. I'm close enough to watch over things, but far enough away that I can't be bothered if I don't want to be found."

If I don't want to be found.

Willa watched him, knowing that there was much more to Lucas Dorsette than he wanted the world to see. He was witty, flirty, a charmer, no doubt. But there was a serious side to him that she could see clearly, in spite of the shaded, secluded garden where he'd brought her. Or maybe because of it.

"Do you bring all your conquests here?" she asked, smiling at him.

"Actually, you're the first," Lucas told her, his

mood as dark and hard to see into as the swamp below them. "Conquest, that is."

And that's when Willa knew she was treading on very dangerous ground. Lorna had warned her about Lucas's lighthearted, carefree nature.

But her friend had failed to warn her about the other qualities that made up Lucas Dorsette. He was obviously a very complex, interesting man. A man who had a deeper, more spiritual side that he hid from the world with a nonchalant shrug and a breathtaking smile.

But then, maybe he didn't want the rest of the world to see that side of him. The side that cared enough to set God's creatures free when he could just as easily destroy them. The side that tended and nurtured a secret, tragic place, finding beauty hidden in the midst of pain. The side that didn't want to be found.

Taking all that into consideration, Willa stopped asking questions and quit worrying about being his next conquest. Instead, she sat next to him on the carved bench inside the pagoda. Sat in silence, listening to the sounds of the swamp, the starlings fussing as they flew overhead, the bullfrogs singing in the marsh. Listening to the soft, sweet melody of hundreds of tiny chiming bells.

Across the shore, a blue heron posed on a toppled branch from a bald cypress tree, listening and watching right along with them. And somewhere in the coolness of the swamp, a mourning dove cooed a forlorn song of longing.

"Thank you for showing me this place, Lucas," she told him after a few minutes.

"Thank you for letting me bring you here," he replied, his tone neither carefree nor careless. Instead, his husky voice held a reverent longing of its own.

Which made her wonder all over again.

Why had he opened up to her, let her see the real Lucas Dorsette, here in this ancient, tragic spot, of all places on God's green earth?

"Set another place for dinner," Lorna told Rosie Lee that afternoon. "Willa O'Connor will be joining us."

Lucas walked in the kitchen in time to hear this bit of news. "Willa? Well, I think the dinner hour just got more interesting. Glad I actually dressed."

He'd never admit that he'd taken great pains to get cleaned up in hopes of seeing her here tonight. Crisp button-up shirt, pressed and pleated khaki trousers. Shoes that didn't have scuff marks and caked mud all over them. He'd even found a belt.

"And where have you been since breakfast?" Lorna asked him as she opened the oven to check on Rosie Lee's baked turkey cutlets. "Willa came back to the house without you. Did you do something to upset her?"

"Which question would you like me to answer first?" he asked, perturbed that his baby sister had automatically jumped to the wrong conclusion. And she hadn't even noticed that he'd tried to clean up nicely.

"You did do something, didn't you?"

Giving Lorna a direct look that matched her own assumptions, he nodded. "Yes, I sure did. I kidnapped her and took her deep into the swamp and then—"

"Oh, hush up," Aunt Hilda said, coming into the kitchen at a slow pace, one hand leaning heavily on her cane. "I can tell you where Lucas was today, Lorna. He spent most of the afternoon with me at the office, handing out school supplies to the area children."

"School supplies?" Lorna adjusted her chef's hat, then shrugged. "Will wonders never cease."

"I even went into Kenner to that big superstore and bought them, too," Lucas told her. "Can you believe Aunt Hilda assigned me such a monumental chore?"

Lorna stuck out her tongue at him. "Yes, I can believe it. And I'm well aware of the local effort to help our children with their supplies this year. Between the tornado and then the flood, we all know everyone around here is tapped out, both emotionally and financially."

"That's right," Aunt Hilda said, placing an arm around Lucas's shoulder. "School will be starting in a few weeks, and we need to do everything we can to make it a normal transition, in spite of all the havoc nature has created this year."

"Okay," Lorna said. "But that still doesn't explain why Willa came back to the house by herself."

"I escorted her to the garden—the official garden," Lucas explained. "She wanted to go to her room, so I bid her good day, then I went on my merry way.''

And wished he could have stayed in his secret garden with Willa for, oh, maybe the rest of his life.

He couldn't explain what had happened this morning. He only knew he'd needed to take Willa to that particular spot. Call it instinct, call it a need to let her into his secret hopes and dreams. Or call it a coward's plea for someone to see inside his soul, but Lucas had been sure and solid in his decision.

And…she'd understood.

Willa hadn't questioned him. She hadn't condemned him. She'd sat there with him, in the quiet of the summer morning, with the bayou and the birds and bees all around them. And she'd…accepted.

Lucas had been around many beautiful women, too many, when he really stopped to think about it. But none of them had ever accepted him for what he was. They'd all wanted to dig too deep, wanted more than he could give. They'd all tried to corner him, change him, rearrange him into fitting husband material. Which only made him bolt right out the door.

Maybe it was because she was worldly and world-weary, but Willa didn't seem to expect a whole lot from him. He supposed that could be good or bad, depending on how you looked at things. Maybe Willa didn't expect too much because she'd hardened herself to men in general.

Or maybe she knew he couldn't possibly live up to her expectations.

Lorna brought that point home with her next statement. "Well, I thought you were going to keep an eye on Willa, watch over her while she's here."

"I would gladly do that," he responded, reaching into Rosie Lee's spinach salad to snare a fat slice of green pepper. "But Willa said she was tired and she was going back to her room to rest and make a few phone calls. So I left her to it."

And wondered why she'd looked so sad as she'd walked away.

Lorna frowned, then nodded. "Okay, then. I know she didn't let anyone know where she'd be, not even her agent. And I think she's turned off her cell phone. I hope she did get some rest today." Glancing at the clock, she added, "Oh, I've got to get to the restaurant before Mick gets home. Just as soon as I gauge the crowd and make sure my assistant and Em can handle things, I'll be back for dinner."

"We'll be honored by your presence," Lucas teased.

Lorna gave him a mock-nasty glare, then reached to kiss him on the cheek. "I'm sorry I jumped on you, brother."

"What else is new?"

"You're still my favorite brother, you know."

"Maybe because I'm your *only* brother."

She smiled at him, all trace of doubt gone. "I want you to be happy, Lucas."

"But just not with your fair friend Willa."

"I didn't say that. Actually, it would be nice if—"

Willa came into the room then, her crystal-blue eyes bright and red-rimmed, her expression bordering on frantic. In spite of that, she looked glorious in a long, straight blue cotton sundress etched with embroidered daisies on its wide crisscrossed straps.

Lucas started to question her but glanced at his sister and saw the warning look in Lorna's worried eyes.

He turned to Willa, hoping to lighten her mood. "I hear you're joining us for dinner. Most of the guests eat in the restaurant, so we're glad to have you at our table."

"Thank you," she said, her words just above a whisper. "I hope I won't be intruding on a family gathering."

"Not at all," Aunt Hilda told Willa, her sharp gaze taking in everything. "As Lucas said, we don't provide dinner for our guests—just breakfast. But Lorna figured out a way around that with her booming restaurant."

Lucas grinned, then took his aunt by one arm as he extended the other to Willa. "But we never turn down a beautiful face at the dinner table, either, when the occasion presents itself."

He waited, saw Willa hesitate, wondering. He wanted to pull his hands through her haphazardly upswept hair.

Then she put her arm around his, lifted her head and gave him a brilliant smile that would probably sell lots of lipstick in a magazine shot. "How can I refuse, then?"

How, indeed, Lucas wondered. She seemed anything but eager to have dinner with his family. She seemed sad and forlorn, just like his lost, forgotten garden in the bayou.

Lucas wanted to wipe away her tears, make her smile again, from the heart. But first he had to find out what had brought her here and why she seemed so fragile.

As he walked with his aunt and Willa up the central hallway of Bayou le Jardin, Lucas knew one thing for sure.

God had brought Willa to him. And Lucas had been right to take her to his private garden.

It was the place where he kept his fears and sadness intact, nurturing them as if they were cherished blossoms lost deep inside the swamp.

He looked at Willa and knew that beneath her pain, the beauty was still there, just as with his garden. He felt an acute need to clear away the bramble and entanglements surrounding Willa's smile and bring that beauty into the light.

Chapter Four

Lucas flipped on the light by his favorite armchair in the little den off the kitchen. "Well, well. Would you look at that?"

"I knew you'd want to see it," Rosie Lee told him, shaking her head. "Dem fellows might be back, Lucas."

"Yeap, they just might. And I just might be waiting for them."

Lucas focused on the supermarket tabloid Rosie Lee had handed him. The supermarket tabloid that had a picture of Willa O'Connor, standing on the bayou, plastered across its front cover, complete with the headline "Supermodel flees New York for bed-and-breakfast retreat in Louisiana." Then, in a subhead, "Why did Willa O'Connor cancel her appearance in benefit fashion show? Details inside."

Lucas wanted the details. But not this way. He wanted Willa to tell him what was going on. If she saw this, she'd probably pack up and head for parts unknown.

Because she was obviously running from something.

Lucas knew this because, hey, it took one to know one. He'd certainly run away a few times in his life. To the swamp. To New Orleans. To his garden pagoda. He could see all the signs.

But why had Willa come here?

Maybe because she needed to be here; God wanted her to be here right now. Last night at dinner, she'd been polite—her manners were impeccable. She'd also been aloof and withdrawn, traits expected of a haughty model, but they didn't fit the Willa he'd seen when they'd been alone in the garden. There she'd been more open, more down to earth. Lucas wished he could figure out the real Willa O'Connor, not the glossy image she'd managed to project both on paper and in the flesh.

He put down the tabloid, telling himself he wouldn't read the disgusting and obviously untrue article inside. Then he pulled out the worn picture he'd found of Willa in the fashion magazine the other morning, comparing it to the blurry headshot from the tabloid.

There was no comparison.

In the glossy magazine shot, Willa looked picture-perfect as she stood smiling on a bridge in Venice, wearing a shimmering baby blue satin evening gown and dazzling jewels. It was an ad for a very expensive designer perfume. It worked for him.

In the tabloid picture, Willa looked lovely, but she

had that same lost, worried look on her face Lucas had noticed so many times in the past two days. She was staring at the water as if hoping to find answers there. The intrusive photographers had captured her in a very private moment. And they'd obviously had more than one roll of film, since Lucas had destroyed the rolls in their cameras.

That *didn't* work for Lucas.

He wanted to find those two clowns and grind them both to pulp. But Aunt Hilda would tell him that wasn't the way a Dorsette resolved conflict.

So did he pray for their rotten, misguided souls instead?

Better to pray for Willa. To pray that he could find a way to get closer to her, help her through whatever problem she'd come here to solve.

Rosie Lee stuck her head in the doorway. "Want more coffee, Lucas?"

"Non." He got up, threw the trashy tabloid on the worn coffee table. "I'm going out to find the rest of the breakfast crowd. Then I've got a busy day—got to check the dip nets and trotlines so Lorna will have fresh seafood for dinner tonight. Then I'm supposed to get with Mick and Justin to go over the renovation plans for later this fall. But first I need to see—"

"Willa O'Connor is out on the gallery," Rosie Lee told him with a grin.

It was uncanny the way Rosie Lee could read his mind, Lucas thought as he grabbed his cup of now cold coffee and headed through the kitchen to the back gardens. Glancing over the clusters of people eating their morning meal, Lucas saw a couple of new faces.

And the one face he'd been searching for.

They were booked solid for the summer, in spite of the damage from the storms earlier in the spring. Of course, Justin and the whole clan had worked around the clock to get the house and gardens in order, but there was still a lot that needed to be done, which was why they would probably have to shut down for a couple weeks in the less busy late fall.

Upkeep on the place was a never-ending battle, but one they gladly accepted. Lucas had pitched in, too. He loved these gardens and their home as much as his aunt and sisters did.

And right now, he especially loved having Willa O'Connor sitting at a wrought-iron table in beige linen pleated slacks and a stark black sleeveless summer sweater, her long hair pulled from her classic face with an exotic metal and wooden clip, her face devoid of any makeup. She looked as if she belonged in a country garden.

As always, her natural beauty assaulted Lucas with the same force as the many flowers blooming around them. It slammed into his gut with a gentle rendering, making him inhale then exhale in one quick breath. He didn't understand this attraction, had never had to deal with anything quite so strong and sure before. He'd been attracted to other women, but he'd never felt a jolt that went all the way from his stomach to his toes.

And he'd never felt such a fierce longing, a mixture of wanting to protect her and nurture her coupled with a need to know everything about her.

"Staring is quite rude," Aunt Hilda said under her breath as she walked past him. She took the time to stop and rap his leg with her cane before she moved on, a twinkle in her eyes. "I'm going to work. And you, try to stay out of trouble."

Lucas snapped to attention, then realized he wasn't the only one staring at Willa. An older couple sitting at the next table—the Gilberts from East Texas— were whispering and staring. And Mrs. Gilbert had a copy of that annoying tabloid in her plump little hand.

Lucas saw the ambush coming before he could take a step to warn Willa.

"It is you, isn't it?" Mrs. Gilbert chirped as she fluttered to her feet and rushed to Willa's table. "See. It says so right here." She pointed to the picture, then looked at Willa, smug and proud of her discovery. "I told William I thought this was you. The story says you didn't show up at an important fashion event. Says you're having personal problems."

Lucas watched as Willa's smile turned to stony surprise. "I beg your pardon?"

"Honey, it's okay, really," Mrs. Gilbert said, leaning close. "I can understand why you'd want a little downtime. I mean, traveling to all those exotic places, wearing all those beautiful, costly clothes at fashion shows." She made a shushing sound, then rolled her eyes. "I wish I had it so hard." She beamed a smile at Willa. "Did you really walk away from a cancer benefit fashion show in New York last week?''

Willa looked at the tabloid picture, then turned as pale as the ice in her freshly squeezed orange juice. ''Where did you get this?''

''The drugstore in town,'' Mrs. Gilbert replied, nodding. ''Went in for some sunscreen and just had to have this, too. I love catching up on all the gossip.'' She pulled a pen from the pocket of her cotton tunic. ''Will you sign it for me?''

Willa got up so fast, she knocked over the juice. ''I'm sorry,'' she said, looking around. ''I...''

''I think Miss O'Connor isn't in the mood to sign any autographs right now,'' Lucas said, coming to stand by Willa, his arm gently nudging her so she could lean against him. ''She didn't give permission for that picture to be published, and the article is a complete fabrication. Well, you understand, of course, Mrs. Gilbert. There's no big story here. Miss O'Connor just wants some privacy.'' He flashed the older woman one of his best smiles. ''Isn't that the very reason you and Dr. Gilbert keep coming back to Bayou le Jardin year after year—just to get away from all the stress of running a private practice and those fussy patients? You know how we pride ourselves on keeping our guests happy.''

Mrs. Gilbert looked embarrassed, then she smiled at Lucas. ''Of course, Mr. Dorsette. Wouldn't have it any other way.'' She shrugged. ''It's just that, well, a supermodel, right here at breakfast. It's not every day you find that.''

''I agree,'' Lucas said, his hand squeezing Willa's

arm. Her skin felt silky soft, but cold in spite of the heat. "Miss O'Connor, have you met Mrs. Gilbert? Margaret Ann Gilbert and her husband, Dr. William Gilbert. They've been coming to Bayou le Jardin every summer for several years now. Two of our favorite guests."

"Oh, my," Mrs. Gilbert said, playfully slapping Lucas on the arm as she batted her eyelashes at him. "It's so very nice to meet you, Miss O'Connor. My, you're so tall."

Willa gave Lucas a grateful look, then reached out to shake Mrs. Gilbert's hand. "I'm sorry if I acted rudely, Mrs. Gilbert. It's just that I thought I'd have some privacy here, and seeing that picture—"

"It's not a very clear shot, is it?" Mrs. Gilbert replied, obviously enjoying Willa's discomfort.

Dr. Gilbert, a tall man with a tuft of white hair, came ambling over to take his petite wife by the arm. "Margaret Ann, I declare, can't you see the woman doesn't want to be bothered? Now stop gawking and come on back to our table and eat your breakfast. Lorna made these cinnamon rolls especially for you, dear."

"Yes, I certainly did," Lorna said, getting up to find more of the freshly baked concoctions. Emily came rushing out of the kitchen with a steaming batch. "Look, here's Em with more. Have another, then take a nice stroll around the gardens. The butterfly garden is especially pretty this time of year."

Mrs. Gilbert gave Lorna and Willa an envious stare. "Well, I shouldn't have any more, but I suppose I'll never be supermodel thin like the two of you. Might as well enjoy myself in my old age, huh?''

''Exactly,'' Lucas told her as he let go of Willa to escort Mrs. Gilbert to her table. Then he leaned low to whisper in the captivated woman's ear. ''And thank you for understanding about our special guest. You are such a discreet person, I hope I can count on you to know exactly the right thing to say—if anyone asks about Willa being here, that is.''

''Oh, my, of course,'' Mrs. Gilbert said as Lucas gently pushed her into her chair. ''William, pass me another roll, sweetheart.''

''Of course, honey,'' Dr. Gilbert said, a twinkle in his eyes. ''Think I'll have another myself, too.''

Lucas left them smiling and cooing over Lorna's fluffy iced cinnamon rolls, their coffee cups filled to the brim with a fresh brew, thanks to Emily. Lorna gave Lucas a thankful look, then headed over to entertain and distract the Gilberts.

''Thank you,'' Willa said as he drew near. ''I appreciate that.''

She still looked pale and shaken.

''Why don't you sit back down,'' Lucas told her. He indicated her chair. ''Do you want something else? Some more juice?''

She sank into her chair. ''No, no. I'm fine, really. Seeing that picture just startled me. I didn't want anyone to know—''

''That you're here.''

She nodded, then looked at him. ''And that I didn't live up to a commitment. I've never backed out of a show in my life, especially when it's a charity event.''

Lucas snagged a crisp piece of bacon Lorna had left on her plate. ''Couldn't be helped, I reckon.''

''I should have gone through with it, but I did have my reasons for being a no-show,'' Willa replied, more to herself than to him. ''I'd hate to think—I don't want people to believe—''

''People will believe what they want to believe,'' Lucas interjected, his hand on hers. ''You've obviously got a good reason for deciding to cancel out on the show.''

She looked up. ''But you don't believe me, either, do you? I can see it in your eyes. You're wondering exactly what the rest of the world is wondering—how could I be so shallow and self-centered?''

She jumped up to stare down at him.

Lucas caught her before she could bolt for the house. ''Hey, now, slow down. Yes, I'm wondering what happened. But I refuse to believe gossip or half-truths. What I'd really like is for you to talk to me, tell me what's bothering you.''

She lowered her head. ''I can't.''

''Why not? You can trust me.''

Willa pulled her arm away. ''It's not about trust. This is something I have to deal with on my own, in my own way. I just need some time to think things through, make a decision.''

''And you'd rather be left alone?''

Her expression told him one thing, but her eyes told him that she needed someone to help her through whatever crisis she was dealing with.

"I have to resolve this on my own terms, Lucas," she replied. She reached a hand up to absently scratch a bright red spot on her arm. Then she turned to leave.

Lucas moved like lightning to catch up with her. "What's wrong with your arm?"

She shrugged, refusing to look at him. "Nothing. Just a few bug bites from our excursion into the swamp the other day. I've got some lotion in my room."

"Oh, no," he said, pulling her toward the French doors. "Rosie Lee has this stuff she makes up herself with herbs and witch hazel. It'll take the sting out. C'mon, we'll find it. These Louisiana mosquitoes can be fierce."

She smiled. "It does itch."

"We'll fix it," Lucas told her, taking her into the kitchen.

Rosie Lee glanced up from the industrial-size dishwasher. "Can I get you anything, Lucas?"

"Nah. We're just gonna head into the sitting room to doctor Willa's bug bites."

Rosie Lee nodded, then turned to her work. "Poor *bébé*. You're sure too pretty for da mosquitoes to tote off, for true."

"Thank you," Willa said, smiling at the other woman.

Emily came in and glanced shyly at Willa. "Miss O'Connor, I just love…I love seeing you in all the magazines. I can't believe you're really here."

Willa gave the teenager a soft smile. "Thanks, Emily. Just remember, what you see in the magazines is the product of a whole team of people—makeup artists and hairstylists, not to mention the marketing and advertising gurus. I know it might sound trite, but real beauty comes from within. And your pretty smile shows me that you have an inner beauty all your own.''

Emily blushed, looked at her mother, then shook her head. "But I'll never look like you."

"You weren't meant to," Willa replied. "Just be yourself. You have beautiful olive skin and glorious dark hair. Would you believe, I used to wish I had dark hair like yours?"

"Non," Emily said, laughing. Then she touched her rich brown locks. "It *is* natural."

"Keep it that way, suga'," Lucas interjected with a wink. "Em, you know you're the belle of Bayou le Jardin, don't you, now?"

"Lucas, you're teasing me," Emily said, grinning.

But Lucas saw the way she held her head high. Willa's praise had given the young woman some much-needed confidence.

"Em, get back to your chores," her mother said softly, a look of pride on her face.

Emily rolled her eyes, then grinned again. "I'll see you later."

"Medicine's on the shelf in the pantry," Rosie Lee told Lucas. Then she glanced at Willa. "Thanks for talking to her. She's at that age where she thinks she's ugly. Me, I think she's the prettiest thing in the world, but I'm just her mamma, *hein?*"

"She is pretty," Willa replied. "She'll blossom into a beauty soon."

"*Oui,* her papa is worried about that very thing."

While Rosie Lee went back to work, Lucas tugged Willa into the little sitting room. "There," he indicated, placing her on the couch, his gaze holding hers. "That was a very nice thing you just did."

Willa shrugged, then looked away. "What? Talking to Emily? I was telling her the truth. She's at such a hard age—caught between baby fat and hormones. I certainly can remember those days."

Lucas let his gaze move over her slender frame. "Did you actually ever have any baby fat?"

"Yes, I sure did. But I was all arms and legs, so awkward and gangly. I felt like an ugly duckling."

"And turned into a beautiful swan."

He saw the sadness falling across her like a cloud over the sun.

"Where's this soothing medicine?" she asked, her eyes on her itching bite. She rubbed it with obvious nervousness. To avoid looking at him, he guessed.

After rummaging through the first aid kit in the pantry that connected the sitting room with the kitchen, Lucas found the antiseptic lotion that Rosie Lee kept handy for just such purposes.

"Ah, here it is," he told Willa, coming to sit on the footstool in front of her. Noticing the tabloid on the table, he quickly shoved it to the floor before she had a chance to see it.

Then he took her arm in his hand and began to rub creamy, fresh-scented medicine on the swollen bite. "That ol' skeeter got you bad, love. Does it still sting and itch?"

Willa looked at him, her big blue eyes filled with

gratitude and resolve. "It's not that bad. I've got a couple of others, mostly on my legs. I'll doctor those with Rosie Lee's medicine later, if you don't mind."

"I could do those, too," he teased, glad to see a smile tugging at her beautiful lips. "I guess in your profession, you have to be extra careful about bug bites and scrapes—the camera probably isn't too kind to injuries."

She nodded, her thick ponytail falling over her shoulder. "I have to be careful, but we have the magic of airbrushing and touching up the photos to help us look perfect—even when we're not."

"You're as close to perfect as any woman I've ever met," Lucas said, his hand going still on her arm. "I just need to take better care of you next time we venture out."

"I can take care of myself," she reminded him. "You need to stop coming to my rescue all the time. And you also need to understand that I'm far from perfect."

Lucas sat back, his fingers touching her arm, his other hand still holding her steady. "Okay, I'll accept that you probably have your failings, whatever they might be, but I *like* rescuing you. And besides, I'm a highly trained professional. I took a six-week course at Tulane University on how to handle damsels in distress."

"Funny, I didn't know Tulane offered such a course."

"They only let certain people go through it." He winked, grinned, then continued to rub her arm. "And they prepare us for lovely, long-limbed models. They warn us that we might lose our hearts, so we have to be strong and prove our worth. It's a tough challenge—only for the very brave. But we take our job very seriously.''

''You're completely crazy,'' she told him, scoffing. ''How many women have you told that tall tale, anyway?''

''I don't go around rescuing every woman who comes around that big curve in the road,'' he told her, serious. ''But…you're different, Willa. It seems as if I'm just supposed to be here for you.''

She abruptly pulled her arm away. ''I don't need anyone to be here for me, Lucas. I've been on my own for a very long time.''

''And why is that?'' he countered, ignoring the way she'd successfully cut off any shred of intimacy between them.

''I'm adopted,'' she blurted. Then she lowered her head, as if ashamed.

Lucas lifted her chin with his thumb. ''What's that got to do with anything?''

Looking up, she said, ''My parents were older than most when they decided to adopt a child. My father is an ambassador—to a small country halfway around the world. And my mother…she always followed my father around, clinging to him, hoping to be the best possible wife she could be. But she couldn't have children, and my father wanted a child more than anything. I think that's the only reason she agreed to an adoption, because he wanted it so much. They both needed a child for appearances' sake.''

Lucas thought that was a terrible thing to think about your own parents, and especially about yourself. That brought thoughts of his dead mother and father and how much they had treasured their three children. Pushing bittersweet memories away, he held Willa, his hand cupping her face. "Why do you think that, *chère?*"

Willa didn't try to twist away. Instead, she leaned into his touch. "They were so distant, so formal when I was growing up. They still are. And they expected so very much, more than I was ever able to give."

"Do you see them now? I mean, are they still alive?"

"Oh, yes, I see them during holidays—the obligatory visit. But they travel here and there with the social set, their image intact in spite of their daughter's disgraceful antics."

"I don't see anything disgraceful in this face," he told her, inching closer.

"I was supposed to be just like my mother," she explained, her expression grim. "I went through boarding school, prep school, college. Then I was supposed to marry some Ivy Leaguer with plenty of old money and settle down to charity events and committee work."

"I guess that didn't happen."

"No. I was 'discovered' when a modeling scout came to our campus to do some photo shoots. A friend talked me into going to the shoot just for fun. Well, the agency rep seemed to like me, but at first, I resisted the offer. I'm not one to be impulsive, you see. But the scout and the agency were very persistent. Signed me up on the spot a week before graduation.

"I think I agreed just to spite my parents and their latest catch, a very eligible bachelor who met all their credentials. It was a way to run away, get away. When I turned down his marriage proposal and told my parents I was heading to France for my first modeling assignment, they practically disowned me."

"But you're famous, rich, accomplished. What's the matter with these people?"

"I've asked my therapist that many times," she said, her smile warming his hand. "And I've longed to know what's wrong with me just the way I am." She stopped smiling. "Then, after I informed them I wanted to find my real mother—"

Lucas watched as she became silent again. He saw the pain marring her face, felt it in the touch of his fingers to her skin. "Did you—find her, I mean?"

Willa put her hand over his, pulling it away from her face. "I've been searching for so long. I had just about given up. But about a month ago, the private investigator I hired came up with a family name and a location. Now I'm trying to get up the courage to go and see if this family might be my family."

"Wow." He held her hand in his. "So…what's holding you back?"

Her eyes misted over, but she held the tears at bay.

"I'm afraid," she finally admitted. "I'm so afraid of what I might find if I do go to see my real mother. What if she doesn't want to see me?"

"That would be tough," he said, nodding. "But if this is something you have to do—"

"It is." She got up, the aloof nature intact once again. "Thanks for the medicine. The itching's stopped now."

"Willa, wait." He rose to go after her. But she was already in the hall, heading up the winding stairs. "Willa, do you want to talk about this?"

"No," she told him, turning to stare at him. "Thanks, Lucas. But there's so much more to the story. And I really can't explain all of it right now."

"When?" he asked, his heart hurting for her. "When, Willa?"

"I honestly don't know," she said. "And I don't think I should stay here too much longer. It's only going to get worse if I do." With that, she turned and fled up the stairs to the second floor, shutting her bedroom door behind her.

Lucas turned from the stairs to look out the French doors, his gaze scanning the great oaks surrounding the front of the house. "How could it get any worse?" he wondered out loud.

After all, he'd already lost his heart.

He could be persistent. He would find out what Willa was so worried about, what secrets she'd brought to Bayou le Jardin with her.

And he'd gladly help her to find her long-lost biological mother, if she'd let him. Because he wasn't about to let Willa leave these gardens in her current state of mind. Nor anytime soon, if he had his way.

And Lucas Dorsette always got his way.

Chapter Five

"I let you get away with this one, Willa, but if you keep pulling these stunts your career is going to be in serious jeopardy."

Willa held the cell phone tightly to her ear, the warning words from her agent reminding her that her life was falling apart even as she sat here.

"I understand that, Samuel. But I need a little more time. I'm exhausted, worried, confused. I have to have a few more days, at least."

She sank back on the antique white wicker chair, one hand digging into the soft, plush floral cushion as she looked from the second floor gallery to the gardens below. Contrasting the peaceful, bucolic scene spread out in front of her with the impatient sigh of her longtime agent, Samuel Frye, only made Willa more conscious of her obligations and commitments.

"If you'd just let me in on what's going on with you," Samuel said, his words etched with exasperation as well as concern. "Willa, you are one of my best clients. We've made a whole lot of money together, me and you. You're wholesome, the girl next door, and you aren't a prima donna. So I don't get this—"

"You mean, I'm acting like a prima donna now," she interjected, her gaze scanning the distant row of hot-pink and fuchsia-colored crape myrtle trees Lucas had tugged her through a couple of days ago. Putting thoughts of Lucas and their time together out of her mind, Willa tried to find a reason to give Samuel for her refusal to come back to New York. "Samuel, have I ever embarrassed you? Have I ever before backed out on any of my contracts or my commitments? Haven't I worked hard for you?"

"Yes, of course."

She could almost see Samuel's distinguished, cratered face. He'd been in the business for so many years some of the younger models called him Papa Frye. Samuel didn't mind the title one bit. In fact, he encouraged it. He had a big heart, and he took care of his clients, especially the young women who were thrust into the sophisticated world of fashion modeling at such early ages. He set high standards for himself and his clients. Willa didn't want to let him down.

"Maybe you're right," she said at last. "I'm not really accomplishing anything here, and unfortunately, that tabloid story is only going to alert the rest of the media as to my whereabouts. I know I can't stay here much longer without more questions popping up, but there is something I have to take care of before I can come home.''

"But you do plan on coming home soon, to help me try to do some damage control regarding this benefit show?''

Willa looked over the gardens toward the bayou. She'd seen Lucas heading toward the restaurant and boathouse earlier, had watched as he'd steered his pirogue into the brown-black waters of the swamp. He'd disappeared in a low mist, like some figment of her imagination.

She wanted to escape and run after him, to ask him to take her into that lush landscape so she could hide from the world, hide from her responsibilities and her doubts. She was so very tired.

But Willa knew that would be a mistake.

"I just need until the weekend,'' she told Samuel. "That's three more days. I don't have anything pressing anyway for a couple of weeks.''

Samuel sighed again. "Okay. I'll hold off any bookings other than the ones we already have scheduled until I hear from you on Monday. But I expect you to be back in New York by then. And…I expect you to tell me what this is all about. You know I'm only here to help, Willa. If you need anything…''

"You're a sweetheart,'' Willa replied, wishing she could explain things to him. "Listen, I'll be here through the weekend, but I know I've got to move on to avoid the press. And I've got some personal things to take care of. So…you have my cell number. You can track me down if something urgent comes up. But, Samuel, I'd really appreciate it if you could just back off for a while."

"Okay, all right. I've sent out a press release explaining why you had to pull out of the benefit show—exhaustion, fatigue, the usual. I only hope people don't think—"

"That I'm sick, that I'm hooked on drugs or alcohol?" She shook her head even though Samuel couldn't see her. "We both know that's not true."

"Yes, we know that, but you have to understand how the press takes these things. Just like that two-bit tabloid, they make up what they can't prove."

Willa closed her eyes, letting the tiredness wash over her. "Yes, I know. But I need some privacy. I need to work through this without the press hovering around. I'll be in touch."

With that, she hung up, then tossed the phone on a nearby white wicker table.

How could she ever explain this to anyone?

She thought of Lucas, remembering his gentle touch this morning as he'd doctored her bug bites. He was such a kind man. So different from any man she'd ever been involved with.

Was she becoming involved with Lucas Dorsette?

Willa closed her eyes, wondered how to pray. She'd never been taught how to talk to a higher source, had never been encouraged to attend church on a regular basis. Her parents, so aloof, so worldly, had been inclined to look on religious practices as something to be tolerated, something to be used when time and circumstances called for it. As far as she knew, they didn't even attend church.

Then Willa thought of Lucas and his sisters, of Aunt Hilda and the Babineaux family. All so devout, all so sincere and secure in their faith.

Why did she feel so safe with them? With Lucas?

She didn't want to depend on him. She'd always depended on herself. Knowing she'd been adopted caused her to put up a shield around herself—distancing her heart from the tormenting questions that had always haunted her.

Did her real mother love her? Had she been forced to give up her child? Did her adopted parents really love her, or had they only taken her in to put up a facade of being the perfect family?

Lucas had lost his parents so long ago. Her heart went out to him. How he and his sisters must have suffered. And yet they carried on. They believed God would show them the way.

She got up to stand at the intricate iron and wood railing, a railing that had been forged and created right here on this land long ago, according to Lacey.

Tradition. Heritage. Roots. Family.

Willa longed to have those things, not a nomadic facsimile. She was plain tired of running from the truth. And she knew that healthwise, her own time might be running out.

She closed her eyes again, tried to form the words to ask the God she didn't really know or understand to help her find her path in life.

And then she opened her eyes and looked down to find Lucas standing under a great oak tree, staring at her. Her heart stopped, lifted out in the wind to fill with a great, heavy longing.

"You look like a princess in her tower, standing there, love," he called to her.

Willa leaned over the balcony, waving at him. "Are you my prince, come to rescue me yet again?"

"I just might be, at that." Then he lifted himself off the tree's ancient trunk, his head tilted back as he smiled up at her. "Or maybe that should be the other way around. Maybe you've come to rescue me."

Willa wondered what he meant by that statement. He did seem in need of some sort of emotional rescue. But at other times he seemed content, living here far from the madding crowd. She could almost be content here herself.

Except I can't stay. Except you don't know the truth about me.

She should have shouted those words at him.

But she didn't.

Because it suddenly occurred to her that maybe, just maybe, Lucas did need a bit of nurturing companionship, at least. It couldn't hurt to extend the hand of friendship.

If only she had the courage to offer it to him.

Willa wasn't accustomed to rash, impulsive decisions. But something in the mid-morning air urged her to follow her heart just this once. Just for the time she had left here.

"Stay there, my prince," she called, laughing. "I'm coming down from my tower."

Lucas watched as she strolled down the garden path toward him, her smile as radiant as ever. Even if she did have shadows underneath those brilliant blue eyes.

He reached a hand out to her. "Did you get your business taken care of?"

"Yes and no."

"And none of my concern, I suppose."

She shook her head, causing her long ponytail to loop over one shoulder, which only made Lucas want to pull her hair out of its trendy barrette and pull it through his fingers. "No, it's not that. I talked to my agent, and he's fussing for me to come back to New York. Obligations and all of that."

"Ah, obligations." Lucas gave her a quick sideways glance as he tugged her down the path. "We do have to live up to those, don't we?"

"I'm afraid so," she replied. "But I told him I need a few more days here. I'm staying until Sunday, at least."

"Or until the reporters return, at least." He gave her a direct stare, watched as her skin blushed pink. Wondered just what was going through her mind.

"Well, I don't want to involve you and your family in my crazy lifestyle. So, yes, if the reporters return, I'll have to leave sooner."

He tugged her close, bringing her around so he could hold her in his arms. "Then we'd best make good use of the time we have together. Are you afraid of flying?"

She looked puzzled, then amused. "I've flown in airplanes all over the world, Lucas. No, I don't think I'm afraid of flying. In fact, it's become a way of life."

"Oh, really now?"

"Really."

"But you've never flown with *me,* now, have you?"

"Well, no." She grinned, then glanced around as they neared a large white barnlike building, where vehicles and yard equipment were kept. "And I don't recall seeing a plane in the garage."

"Come with me, then," he said, coaxing her toward his Jeep. He had some obligations to fulfill, but that didn't mean she couldn't come along with him.

"Lucas, last time I checked, that was an automobile, not an airplane," she said, pointing toward the sleek black vehicle.

"Yep. That's correct." He opened the passenger side door and bowed gallantly. "Your carriage awaits, milady." When she stood there, he said, "Last time I checked, the private airport on the other side of town had a pretty little single-engine top of the line Ag Cat with my name on it."

"What's an Ag Cat?"

"A crop-dusting plane."

"You're teasing, right?"

"Not at all. I do a little aerial application on the side. And a few loopty-loops when the mood hits me. Want to come along for a look-see ride?"

"What's a look-see?"

"I'm going to do a pass over of a soybean field about ten miles from here. It's located between two thickets, so I have to decide if the chemicals can be dumped in such a way as to keep the thickets environmentally sound. Don't want to kill anything but the bad bugs.''

"So, you won't be spraying any chemicals to-day?''

"*Non.* In fact, after I show off my Ag Cat to you in the safety of the hangar, we'll take out another plane—a sweet old Piper Cub J-3 that belonged to Lacey's late husband, Neil. I use the Cub for all the fun stuff.''

He stopped, remembering how touched he'd been when Lacey had given him the plane after Neil's death. But he didn't want to talk about death. Not today. Not with Willa. So he went back to business.

"I couldn't take you along on a for-real spraying. It's illegal, for one thing, and while I'd enjoy being very close to you, we'd be a bit cramped for space, since my Ag Cat is built to precision for only one person. Plus, the chemicals are nasty.'' He twisted his nose, then made a face. "Gets to the old breathing system if you don't wear protective clothing and a respirator.''

Rolling her eyes, she said, "And you enjoy doing this? Inhaling chemicals in midair?''

"I adhere to all the safety precautions. That's one reason I decided to become a crop duster—so I could keep an eye on the environment around here and try to control what chemicals are dumped and sprayed—and yes, I do enjoy it. It's all in the calculation, you see. The weather, the wind, the lay of the land, they all play a part in the whole thing. When everything is in place, I just drop and dump.''

Willa shook her head, then glanced down. "I don't

know about this—going up in the clouds with a real barnstormer."

Thinking she was going to turn him down and head to the seclusion of her room, Lucas tugged her ponytail. "I promise you'll be safe—I'm a very good pilot. And you won't be bored."

She hopped up on the seat. "I can't imagine ever being bored with you, Lucas."

"Then let's go. It's a perfect day to see the whole view from up above."

"I'd like that," she said.

Lucas took that as a yes.

He was right. She wasn't bored.

The view was breathtaking, a country canvas of square fields of rich, fluttering green and clusters of all types of houses tucked between forest thickets and lush swamps near the slinking dark ribbon of the Mississippi River. The sky was a clear, warm blue with bursts of billowing clouds here and there over-head, while the carpet of the ever-changing land lay beneath like a giant picnic quilt.

He'd also given her a view of his home in all its splendor. From this height, it looked like a beautiful dollhouse, complete with tiny flowers and trees. The double line of great oaks stretched toward them like two arms opening in welcome.

The bayou stretched and shifted beyond the gardens, its dark waters and bearded cypress trees holding their secrets close. In one quiet cove, a dense clutter of cypress knees held a nest of egrets. The birds sat on the gray-tinged limbs and moss-draped stumps, looking like white flower petals. But the roar of the big bird overhead caused the elegant birds to lift and fly en masse across the black-bottomed bayou.

Willa had been in all types of airplanes, but she'd never felt so alive, so exhilarated. Maybe that feeling of complete freedom and lightness had more to do with the highly skilled pilot at the controls than it did with being in the clouds.

Lucas was an expert, but he was also certainly a daredevil, a combination that made him that much more appealing in her eyes.

He'd promised her some loops and twists.

And he'd given her exactly that.

Lucas apparently liked to live on the edge.

Willa laughed over her shoulder at him from where she sat in the front section. He rewarded her with a brilliant grin. With his dark hair tucked beneath a vintage World War Two aviator cap, he looked even more dashing and dangerous than he did out in a pirogue.

Then her heart dropped to her shaky feet as Lucas tilted the plane into a quick spin, setting it right before she had time to be scared. Willa screamed, both delighted and relieved, as he did what he had earlier explained as a P turn, taking her right over Bayou le Jardin and the surrounding swamps and woods.

"It's a tricky maneuver, because the plane can stall out and you're flying about one hundred feet above the earth. You have to concentrate and have good coordination. But don't worry. I've done about a thousand or so such turns and I had to do about a third of those in flight school just to get my license.''

She'd believed him when he'd told her this inside the hangar, and she believed him now. And she felt completely safe in his capable hands.

Which was amazing.

Willa knew she'd never been one to take chances. She liked everything laid out in an orderly, chronological fashion. Perhaps she'd learned that trait from her precise, carefully in-control mother. Candace didn't make a move unless it was completely calculated. And each move had been one step up the social ladder, one more planned achievement for her mother to celebrate.

Yes, Willa had learned from the best. She'd mapped out her career as a model, grim determination making her want to become the best, to show her parents she could, for one thing, and to prove to herself that she could be self-sufficient, for another.

But in all those years of working and traveling and setting almost unreachable goals for herself, she'd never once felt like this.

Only Lucas could make her feel this way—as if each step she took was like jumping off a cliff into clear blue waters. Jumping without a parachute.

A leap of faith.

Get your head out of the clouds, Willa, she told herself as Lucas banked the purring yellow plane and brought it down for the landing. She reminded herself she'd be leaving here soon; she'd be back in New York, back to globetrotting and working long, grueling hours in what most thought was a very lucrative, glamorous job. Her work was that and more, but was it still enough? And did she have enough time to stop and enjoy living? She was the only one who could find the answers to those questions.

But being with Lucas was making her see her life in a whole different light. And from a very different view.

As her heart settled to a steady rhythm, Willa looked at the sky, of which she'd just so daringly been a part.

And suddenly, she wanted to live. Very much so.

She just didn't know how she was ever going to face all the turmoil in her life in order to be able to do that, at long last.

About an hour later they pulled into the long drive leading to the back gardens of the mansion. After parking the Jeep, Lucas came around to Willa's side to open the door, then leaned in through the open window, his face inches from hers. "What can you imagine with me, then?"

She hadn't said much on the short drive home. He wondered if she was having second thoughts about hanging with him. Maybe he'd scared her off before he'd even had a chance with her.

She blinked. "What?"

"You've been so quiet since we came back down to earth," he said, his need to get inside her head flaring with a liquid warmth. "Earlier, you said you couldn't imagine being bored with me. So what are you imagining right now, *chère?*"

Her eyes turned a sparkling blue, as pure and wide

as the Louisiana sky over their heads. Her luscious mouth parted as she took a quick breath. Then she spoke. "I imagine being with you will always be like a wild airplane ride, with lots of loops and free falls."

He lowered his head just a notch. "And that's a bad thing?"

"No, no." She held his gaze, then placed a hand on his arm. "It's just that… Lucas, I came here to work through some things in my life, to make some decisions about my future—"

"A future that doesn't include any heavy commitments and any flighty flings with a poor Cajun boy?"

She shook her head. "A future that is very unsure right now. It wouldn't be fair to drag you into my problems."

"If you're talking about finding your birth mother—"

"It's more than that. I've just got a lot to deal with and not much time to get it all figured out."

"So I don't fit into the equation?"

"I don't want to fit you into the equation. I hope you understand. It wouldn't be right between us, it wouldn't be fair to you."

He leaned closer. He wanted to kiss her bad, but instinct told him that wasn't such a good idea when she was giving him the proverbial brush-off. "Why don't you let me be the judge of that—unless of course, I'm reading all the signs wrong and you're really not as madly in love with me as I am with you."

She reached up then, to touch a hand to his face, to run a slender, polished nail through his wind-tossed hair. "Lorna told me you fall in love very easily."

He grabbed her hand, brought it to his lips. "My sister should mind her own business. Just because she's finally found her soul mate, she thinks she's the local authority on the rest of this miserable lot."

"She cares about you and she worries about you."

He kissed her fingers one by one and enjoyed the way she blushed, the way she seemed to like his touch. "I can take care of myself. Been doing it for years."

"Can you?" Willa watched as he touched her fingers to his mouth, her eyelashes fluttering softly against her cheeks before she looked into his eyes. Lucas saw the attraction jolt through her as it had pushed through him.

Okay, she did have a point. He was losing control. This could turn out to be more dangerous than any of the other stunts he'd tried.

"I used to think I could handle anything," he admitted as he held her hand against his lips. "But it's different with you. I think...I think I'm scared of you, certainly of what you do to me."

She touched her forehead to his. "Oh, Lucas, I don't think you're afraid of anything. I just think you need to know...you need to be warned...I'm not right for you."

Abruptly, he let go of her hand and backed away. "Then maybe I should be scared. At least, that's what you're trying to tell me." Irritated, he opened the door and tugged her out of the Jeep and right into his waiting arms. "Am I right? Are you deliberately trying to scare me away, Willa?"

He saw the answer in the blue of her eyes. And he also saw the contradiction. She was trying to deny her feelings toward him. Lucas took that as a personal challenge to win her over.

"Answer the question, *chère*," he said, his voice low.

She looked down, her expression full of regret. "Yes, I guess I am. For your own good, Lucas."

The anger flared deep inside him, but he tried to hide it as he shifted her closer in his arms. "I really wish everyone would quit telling me what's for my own good."

"Look, I didn't mean to make you mad. It's just that—"

He didn't let her finish that sentence. He couldn't bear to hear the words. Instead, he gently nudged her against the Jeep so he could wrap his arms around her. Then he kissed her with all the pent-up frustration and long-held need that was raging inside his heart.

With the first touch of their lips, however, his rage turned to relief. She was sweet, soft, yielding, promising. She filled that empty place in his soul, the place he only brought out whenever he visited his lost, forlorn garden. The place he'd often prayed would be healed.

Willa was like that prayer being answered at long last.

When he lifted his head, he couldn't take his eyes

away from her. He could tell the kiss had affected her, too. It was there in the bright hope of her eyes, there in the sweet innocent flush of her skin, there in the soft sigh of her breath on his cheek. She might be able to deny her feelings, but she could never again deny the attraction between them.

Their kiss had pretty much made that a certainty and a fact.

But kisses aside, they had a lot of ground to cover before this was settled between them.

"*Je regrette*—I'm sorry," he told her in a whisper. "It's just that…I really needed to do that. For my own good."

Chapter Six

"So my brother took you up in the Piper this morning."

It was a statement, said with Lacey's soft, cultured Southern drawl.

Willa nodded then glanced around the quaint Garden restaurant, wondering where Lucas had gone off to this time. They'd agreed to meet here for a quiet dinner, but instead of finding Lucas waiting for her, she'd run into his older sister, Lacey.

Sensing a hint of disapproval in Lacey's cool gaze, she said, "Yes, he did. And I have to admit, I enjoyed it way too much."

"Lucas has that effect on people. He thinks we all should just drop everything when the mood strikes and go off into the wild blue yonder. He's very impulsive, I'm afraid."

Willa got the distinct impression she was being reprimanded. Or was it yet another warning for her to stay away from Lucas? His sisters sure were protective, even if they did claim to condemn his wild ways.

Before she could respond, Lorna leaned over the table. "I've already warned her, Lacey."

Wanting to defend Lucas, Willa tossed her hair off her shoulder, then placed both hands on the table. "Would you two stop hovering over me? I can take care of things with Lucas. So you both can stop worrying. I'm not sure whether you're trying to protect me, or your brother *from* me. But I can assure both of you—there is nothing serious going on between Lucas and me."

Lorna took that as her cue to sit with them. "Oh, really? Then why do you look positively dreamy every time we mention his name? And why are you sitting here, waiting for him to walk through that door?"

"Yes, she sure has all the signs," Lacey said, her gaze as still as the quiet swamp waters that ran behind the small building.

"We were supposed to meet here tonight," Willa said, her tone low and level in spite of her fluttering heart. She wouldn't dare tell them that since Lucas had kissed her this morning, she'd counted the hours until she'd see him again. Even while she dreaded seeing him again. Lacey was right. He'd had an effect on her. A profound one.

She'd never been a touchy-feely person, but for some reason she couldn't keep her hands off Lucas Dorsette. She liked the feel of his rough-shaven skin, liked the crisp, springy curls of his dark chocolate hair, liked holding his big, callused hands. Loved looking into his mysterious eyes.

But she had to remember that Lucas flirted with a lot of women. Probably took them all flying in his fancy plane. And he probably kissed all the pretty girls and made them cry, too.

"Another date?" Lacey smiled at her sister, then gave Willa the once-over. "That's three dates with the same woman in three days. He's right on schedule."

Seeing the teasing gleam in both sisters' eyes, Willa relaxed and smiled. "I get the point. Okay. And honestly, let me repeat—there is nothing going on between Lucas and me. We haven't actually had what one would term dates. We're just…friends. He's been showing me around—"

"From several vantage points, I gather," Lorna interrupted, her chef hat bobbing as she moved her head. "I wonder where he'll take you next. There's lots of rooms in the house, several private spots in the gardens and the whole swamp out back to explore. And he'll probably want to take you horseback riding—on that wild animal he calls a horse and keeps on his place out in the bayou. That could turn into a lot of…what one *could* term *dates*."

"Oh, all right, enough," Willa replied. "I did have fun up in the plane—"

Lorna held out a hand. "Yes, we couldn't help but notice the two of you, since Lucas made it a point to fly right over the house and grounds. Show-off."

"I wish he hadn't done that," Lacey said in a rough whisper. Then, horror and embarrassment in her eyes, she looked across the table at Willa. "I'm sorry. I mean—"

Lorna put a hand on her sister's arm, then glanced at Willa. "It's the plane—it makes her think of Neil."

Willa immediately felt like sinking into the polished wooden floor. "Oh, Lacey. I'm so sorry. I didn't mean to bring up bad memories—"

"No," Lacey replied, her blue eyes bright. "I don't have any bad memories. Neil used to take me up in that plane, just the way Lucas did you today. I loved it, loved being with him. Then today, when I heard the roar, saw the plane coming across the sky, for a minute—" She stopped, shook her head. "It was silly of me, to think that Neil—"

"Oh, I am sorry," Willa said again, wishing she'd never left her room. "It must be hard, seeing the plane, remembering all the good times you had with your husband."

Lacey barely lifted her chin. "It is. That vintage plane was my husband's pride and joy. But I'm okay, really. Neil left the plane to me, and I...I wanted Lucas to have it. So I should be used to seeing it up in the clouds by now."

Willa didn't know how to respond. She'd never dealt with such grief. "It is a beautiful plane," she said. "And Lucas keeps it in tip-top shape."

"He'd better," Lacey replied, laughing to hide the tears misting her eyes. "Now, I'd better get back down to the house. I've got so much work to do at the shop. I'll probably be working into the wee hours tonight."

"I'd love to stop by and see some of your antiques," Willa said, glad to be off the subject of Lacey's late husband. "I understand you have some beautiful pieces."

Lacey smiled. "Yes, I'm proud of the shop. But I've been busy all summer trying to find pieces to replace some of the furnishings that got damaged in the flood. We were fortunate that only a few inches of water got into the house, but as you've seen, the downstairs rooms suffered some water damage. We've been working hard to repair it, though."

"Lucas explained to me," Willa said. "It's a beautiful house, and I'm so glad Lorna invited me to come down and see it. I just hope I didn't pick a bad time."

"Of course not. We've had a light summer," Lorna told her, waving a hand at the restaurant's few patrons. "Because of the flooding, we've only booked guests who return each year. And we're planning a full shutdown this fall, so we can get things back in proper order for the holidays and the spring season."

Willa couldn't help but admire the two sisters. "You really are a team, all of you—Aunt Hilda, Lucas and you two."

"And now Mick, too," Lorna said, her eyes going as dreamy as she'd accused Willa's of earlier. "He's out somewhere with Justin. Those two stay busy these days."

"Oh, she's about to get all sappy on us, and I think we've had enough of that for one night," Lacey said, walking toward the door. "I'll see you tomorrow."

"Good night," Willa said, watching as the prim blonde left. Then she turned to Lorna. "I hope I didn't upset her."

"It's all right," Lorna said, getting up to head to the kitchen. "She and Neil were very much in love, and it's been hard these last few years. She gets this way every time Lucas takes the plane up. And she refuses to fly in it anymore."

"I can't imagine that kind of pain," Willa said, a deep, nagging worry grabbing her in the stomach. "I've never known that kind of love. It must be so special."

"It is," Lorna said, holding out her hand to admire her wedding band. "I never thought I could find anyone to love, but God sent Mick, and I thank Him every day for my life with my new husband." Then she glanced over Willa's head to the front door. "Speaking of love and marriage, my handsome brother just walked in the door. And he's headed for your table." With that, she grinned, waved to Lucas, then pivoted toward the kitchen.

Love and marriage. Willa certainly hadn't given much thought to either of those subjects. There had been no room for such notions in her carefully planned, carefully arranged career. But she wouldn't be young and pretty forever. Would she wind up all alone, old and lonely?

If she lived to grow old at all?

The thought, coupled with Lacey's obvious grief over losing her husband, only added to Willa's concerns. Which was exactly why she couldn't get involved with Lucas Dorsette, no matter how much his kisses affected her. Better to stay uninvolved and alone than to risk that kind of pain. Especially when her future was so uncertain.

She looked uncertain, sitting alone in the candlelight. She looked fragile, like a delicate blossom. She looked lovely in her shimmering blue sleeveless sheath, like a summer night full of stars.

Get a grip, Lucas. You're a bad poet on a good day and even worse when your poor heart is filled with newfound love.

Was that what he'd been feeling since he'd kissed Willa? Was that this thing that had jolted throughout his body and kept him humming like a taut guitar string all day long? Was that why he'd stolen two of Aunt Hilda's most beautiful salmon and pink-tinged roses to hand to the woman he planned to have dinner with and maybe spend the rest of his life with?

Now, that was surely something he'd never considered with any other woman.

He knew the odds weren't in his favor. First of all, she was exactly his type—blond and leggy. That usually meant he'd lose interest soon enough. Second, he did have a tendency to fall and fall hard for a pretty face. And that meant this wouldn't last too long—they never did. And last but certainly not least, she couldn't stay here forever. She'd be gone soon, back to that world that seemed so far out of his reach. Back to that world of glamour and fame, a world he didn't dare compete with.

And yet, he dared walk across the almost empty

restaurant to hand her the two rose blossoms with a knightly flourish.

"Lucas," she said on a breath of greeting as she took the lush flowers. "Roses. How pretty." She sniffed them, then lifted her brows in suspicion. "And freshly cut, too."

"Right out of my aunt's summer garden," he said as he unbuttoned his tan linen suit jacket and settled into a chair across from her. "Candlelight becomes you, *chère.*"

"Thank you." She pointed toward his suit. "You didn't have to get all dressed up for me."

"*Oui,* I wanted to get all dressed up for you."

He also wanted to tell her that she was the first. The first to see his secret garden. The first he'd invited to go up in the Piper with him. The first woman to make his heart feel both heavy and light at the same time.

In that regard, she had all the others beat.

But unlike the others, she seemed as uncertain as he felt. The kiss that had bonded them had also caused an awkward, wary distance between them.

And so they sat there, silent and uncertain, smiling and quiet, until Lorna came out of the kitchen. "Ready to order now?"

Lucas didn't take his eyes off Willa. "Whatever the special is, love. Surprise me."

Willa didn't stop looking at him. "I'll have...oh, I don't know. Something light."

Lorna slapped a hand on the forgotten menus, then picked them up. "Okay, then. Got it. Why don't you two carry on with whatever you're doing there. Be back in a few minutes.''

Lucas waved his annoying sister away, his gaze still centered on the woman across the table. "I enjoyed our plane ride today."

"I did, too."

"I've…I've never taken anyone up with me. It's twice as much fun with a copilot."

She looked shocked. "You mean, you haven't taken all your girlfriends for a ride in the sky?"

"Only you, *belle*. Only you."

He couldn't tell from the muted light, but he had a feeling she was blushing. That only made him want to reach across the small round table and touch his hand to her heated skin. But he kept his hands to himself, along with all the crazy feelings tugging at his heart.

Lorna came back with two plates of steaming noodles piled with fat blackened shrimp. Emily followed with bread and butter. "Anything else?"

Lucas saw his sister poking Emily. Lorna seemed to enjoy watching him suffer.

Just to show her he wasn't, he said, "Maybe some bread pudding—that one you make with the white chocolate."

"I'll bring it out later," Lorna replied. "So…we'll just leave you two to your dinner then."

"Uh-huh. Thanks," Lucas replied absently, his attention still on Willa. Waiting for his nosy sister to depart, he cut a slice of the piping hot bread, then buttered it before handing it to Willa. "Sorry I was a bit late. Last-minute phone calls."

She took the bread. Was it just his imagination, or did her fingers brush his on purpose in the exchange? She took a bite, then said, "I thought I was the one with the busy schedule."

The woman would make a great spokesperson for French bread. With her upswept hair and her three strands of pearls, she made chewing seem so classy and intriguing. In fact, she could just sit there and hold the bread, and Lucas would buy it. In spite of the air-conditioning and his lightweight suit, he was beginning to sweat.

"I might not be a fashion plate, but I do have things to get done," he countered, hoping to take his mind off her beautiful lips. "I have all these side businesses—it's like spinning plates. Can't let any of them fall by the wayside."

Willa finished her bread, leaned forward to prop her elbows on the table, then cupped her chin on her clasped hands, her food obviously forgotten. "What kind of side businesses?"

"Oh, a little of dis and dat," he replied in an exaggerated Cajun voice. He snagged a fat, buttery shrimp with his fork and ate it with a long sigh of pleasure. "Crawfishing in the spring, fishing all summer long, shrimping, traps to mend, boats to repair and pamper. Moss gathering."

"Moss gathering?" She twirled flat, creamy noodles onto her fork. "Is that anything like woolgathering?"

He nodded. "Kinda. Only better. We harvest the Spanish moss that grows on the cypress trees and sell it to craft shops and florists—for decorating."

"I never would have thought—" She stopped, dropped her fork on her plate. "There is just so much about you. You continue to surprise me."

"Well, I'm about out of surprises," he replied with a wink and a nod. "I'm just plain ol' Lucas Dorsette, a simple man with very simple needs."

He saw the flicker of wonder in her vivid blue eyes. Heard the husky inflection of her tone. But he didn't miss the confusion in her question. "What *do* you need, Lucas?"

He leaned forward, his hands clasped in his lap to keep from touching her. "Another kiss from you would surely be nice."

She immediately pushed herself back in her chair. "We can't do that again."

"And why not?"

"I…we…"

"I'm listening."

"No, that's the problem." She threw her hands in the air, then let them drop to her lap. "You haven't been listening at all. I can't get involved with you, Lucas."

He figured she was arguing more with herself than with him. He could see the battle in her defiant eyes.

"Give me one good reason why not?"

She took a sip of iced tea, then sat the goblet down, one long finger moving over the condensation on the side of the tall glass. "Well, I'll be leaving soon, probably sooner than soon. And I have no idea where I'll be going from here."

Leaning back in his chair, Lucas crossed his arms

and lifted his brows. "I can fly a plane. I can drive a boat. I even have a horse. I'll find you."

He saw the effect that statement had on her. Panic. Plain and simple.

Keeping her eyes on her tea glass, she said, "Sometimes we don't want to be found."

"Yeah, I know all about that."

"Then you need to understand that I have to—"

"I'll go with you, you know."

That brought her head up. "Go with me where?"

"To find your birth mother. I'll go with you, help you get through the rough spots."

She lowered her gaze again, then pushed her plate away. Staring at her hands in her lap, she said, "I haven't decided if I want to go see her. I'm still debating."

"Well, whatever you decide, I just want you to know I'm willing to help you through this."

Emily came out of the kitchen to bring them their bread pudding. She sat the rich cream-colored dessert down. "Coffee, Lucas?"

Lucas lifted a brow toward Willa. When she shook her head, he took the time to give Emily a patient smile. "*Non.* But thanks, suga'. We're good."

Willa glanced at the teenager, apparently glad for the interruption. "How did the dress turn out?"

Emily giggled, then bobbed her head. "It was perfect. You were right—the pink one looked better than the red one."

"I'm so glad. And I'm sure your mother is much more pleased about you going to the dance now that you've decided to wear a more demure design."

Emily rolled her eyes. "*Non,* it's my papa who's happy. He didn't want me wearing the red—*pas de tout.*"

"I have to agree with him," Willa replied. "The red was gorgeous, but a bit too old-looking for a sixteen-year-old. You'll be the hit of the school dance, I'm sure." Then she added in a conspiring whisper, "Especially since hot pink is the really big color on all the runways this summer."

"I'll start a new trend," Emily said, her expression full of pride. "*Merci,* Willa."

"You're welcome," Willa responded. "Let me know if I can help with your hair and makeup. And remember, Emily, less is more."

The awestruck teen gave Willa a shy smile, then backed away. "And you let me know if you need anything else."

Lucas gazed at the woman sitting across from him. "Apparently, you've been busy coaching our young Em on her wardrobe."

Willa watched as Emily headed into the kitchen. "Just steered her in the right direction. The pink dress is a bit more tame, and it looks great on her."

"You're amazing," Lucas said. "Emily will never forget you for giving her such good advice."

"And I'll never forget her."

Lucas didn't want to think about forgetting or remembering right now. He wanted to get back to the subject they'd been discussing. "Well, about your birth mother." After making sure they were alone again, he spoke softly. "I mean it, Willa. I'll go with you, if you're afraid."

She looked into his eyes. "Why would you want to do that?"

He reached out to her. He put a hand on her arm, just a brush of fingers over skin. And watched as she closed her eyes. "Because I want to take that pain out of your eyes, love. I want to see that smile. The one that's so famous the world over."

"That smile is strictly for the cameras," she said, her voice raw and low. "It's not the real me."

He tugged her forward, his hand gentle on her arm. "Then let me see the real you, Willa. Let me…let me show you how to find the real you again, through God's grace, through what we feel for each other."

"I don't know anything about God's grace. It's too late for me to ask Him for help."

And she certainly wasn't going to admit that she had any feelings for Lucas Dorsette, Lucas decided. Maybe he'd better concentrate on helping her find some peace of mind, at least.

"No, *chère,* it's never too late to turn to God. He's always here in these gardens, He's in the very air we traveled through, the clouds we passed today. You have to know that in your heart."

"My heart hurts, Lucas. My heart can't take anymore pain."

"Then let me help you. Let God help you. He can heal your hurts, Willa."

"And has He healed yours?"

It was a cruel question. And he knew the answer could be just as cruel, if he gave in to his doubts. "I'm here, aren't I? I'm alive. I'm secure in my faith."

She got up, dessert and roses obviously forgotten. "Are you really, Lucas? Is that why you go and sit in that sad old garden? Is that why you test yourself, push yourself to the edge in airplanes and out in the swamp? Is that why you don't ever take anything seriously?"

Well, he was taking this conversation *very* seriously.

He shot up after her as she turned for the door. Seeing the surprised expressions of his sister and Emily, who stood hovering at the kitchen door, Lucas waved them away and followed Willa outside. "Hey, wait a minute. How do you know I'm not serious? What do you know about me, anyway?"

"That's it exactly," she said, spinning on the stone path. "I don't know anything about you except what I've heard. I've been warned to stay away from you. Warned that you'll break my heart."

"And you believe those warnings?"

She held herself, her arms wrapped against her stomach. "No. I don't believe them at all. But there is something you should believe, something you should know about *me*."

He stood back, distancing himself from the need to hold her close. "Oh, and what's that?"

"I have the power to hurt *you*, Lucas. That's why I can't let things go any further between us."

"Why don't you let me be the judge of that? Why don't you relax and...let things happen naturally?"

"Naturally?" She almost laughed. But it was a bitter laugh. "Like sickness and death? Like Lacey suffering through losing her husband, or you suffering through losing your parents?''

''You don't need to worry about that,'' he told her, anger coloring all the other emotions rolling through his mind. ''I've learned to accept that.''

''Have you?'' She turned to go, then twisted to stare at him. ''Well, maybe I'm not so good at accepting the natural course of things. Maybe I still want to be the one in control.''

He reached for her, but she moved away.

''Willa, listen to me. I have my good days and my bad days and so does Lacey—and Lorna, too, for that matter. Death isn't easy, it isn't something you can rationalize or understand. But we're here, we're alive. Shouldn't that count for something?''

''You'd think so, wouldn't you?'' she asked. Then she turned and headed up the path toward the mansion.

Frustrated and completely confused, Lucas turned to stalk into the restaurant. He didn't bother to finish eating, and he sure didn't bother to explain anything to his obviously curious sister. He didn't even stop to visit with the few patrons still lingering.

He went straight to the corner where the piano and saxophone had a permanent spot. Grabbing the sax, he sat down on a stool and thought about what to play. An old blues tune came to mind, but it didn't suit his mood. Lucas needed help tonight, so he turned to the gospels for inspiration.

He played a song that seemed perfect even though it was short and sweet. It was the hymn he'd thought about the day he'd first seen Willa.

''Something Beautiful.''

Lorna came out of the kitchen to listen. A hush fell over the couples scattered here and there at the intimate tables. Lucas played on, his gaze moving toward the big window that opened to the night and the gardens.

Then he saw her.

On the path, bathed in moonlight and star shine, he could see the silhouette of a tall blond woman as she stood listening. Until the song was finished.

And then she turned and walked away.

Chapter Seven

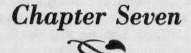

Lucas put down his saxophone, then hopped off the stool centered by the big windows to waylay his sister before she trotted into the kitchen. "We need to talk."

Lorna drew her brows together in a frown. "About what? Or should I say about *whom?*"

"Come and sit," Lucas ordered, gently dragging her to the table he'd shared with Willa. Picking up a fork, he begin stabbing at the bread pudding he'd left.

"Well, I can see your appetite is still intact, even if your poor heart isn't," Lorna said, chin propped on one hand as she gave him a sympathetic smile. "You always did eat your way through misery."

"I'm still hungry," he said. The rich pudding, made of bread soaked in cream and eggs then smothered in rich white chocolate sauce, hit his rattled stomach like nails hitting a tin roof. "Okay, so mebbe this wasn't such a good idea." He pushed the pudding away, then glared at his sister. "What's going on with Willa?"

Lorna waved to some departing customers. *"Bonsoir."* Then she turned to her brother. "Lucas, that's not for me to tell. Willa has been working hard since she was twenty-two years old—since the day she graduated from college—and that's been at least five years. She just needs a break." She shrugged, then removed her chef hat and tossed her tumbling braid over her shoulder. "I met her just before I came back home a little over three years ago—at a posh party in Paris. I was part of the catering team, and she sneaked into the kitchen to get another bite of this fancy chocolate dessert that everyone was raving about."

She stopped long enough to allow Lucas a smile. He commented, "The supermodel sneaking fattening food—now there's a tabloid tale."

"That's about the way it works," Lorna said, bobbing her head. "I caught her gobbling away, and we laughed and ate chocolate cake together. She was very lonely, and I guess I was, too—I was between relationships."

That made him grin. "Wasn't that always the case, love?"

Lorna slapped him gently on the arm, then continued. "Anyway, we had this instant friendship. So we met a couple of days later to go shopping. I told her all about Bayou le Jardin—how I missed it, how I wanted to come home and open my own restaurant. She was so supportive, even offered to be a silent partner if I needed funding." Lorna's expression grew warm with the memory. "I turned her down on the loan, of course. But I did invite her to come and visit."

Lucas leaned forward in his chair. "Why did she wait so long?"

"As I said, she's been very busy. She's in demand, so she's been booked all over the world for fashion shoots and runway work. Over the years, she'd call and we'd chat, catch up, but she was always on her way to some exotic spot. You see, Willa is very disciplined and organized. She had a five-year plan, and I guess she's reached that goal now."

"So you think she decided to just rest a bit?"

Lorna looked at the table, a sure sign that she knew more than she wanted to tell. "I think she needed to stop and regroup."

"And?"

She looked up. "And…that's it."

"Why didn't she come to your wedding?"

"She was in Spain and then she had to go straight from there to Australia. Something about an ad for a sportswear company."

He nodded, then pounced. "So why is she here now? I mean, why is she all of a sudden canceling bookings and not returning phone calls to her agent?"

Lorna rolled her eyes. "You know these things for true?"

"I know what I see." He lowered his voice, his words for her ears only. "Does Willa have some sort of eating disorder?"

Lorna laughed out loud. "Oh, my, *non*." Patting

his hand, she added, "Willa's eating habits are perfectly normal. She's like any other woman in that regard. She loves food but has to watch every bite that goes in her mouth."

Lucas breathed a sigh of relief. "Then she's not sick or anything."

And that's when he saw it. The little flair of apprehension in his baby sister's expressive green eyes.

His heart seemed to go still in his chest. "Lorna?"

Lorna got up, busied herself with clearing away the table dishes. "It's late, brother. Go home and try to get some rest. Mick should be by any minute for a late dinner, then I'm turning in myself."

Lucas stopped her, dishes and all. "Lorna, tell me."

She turned to stare at him, worry coloring her face. "It's not for me to tell, Lucas."

He let her go, then pushed away from the table. "Then I'll just go and ask Willa."

Holding plates to her white jacket, Lorna tried to stop him. "Lucas, please. Don't do that."

But he was already out the door.

On the other side of the huge, sprawling gardens, Willa sat on a bench in a pretty white Victorian gazebo, the scent of trailing wisteria and running roses mingling around her.

Although her bedroom was lovely, she hadn't been able to go to the isolation of that particular place. So she'd walked through the narrow footpaths, letting the moonlight guide her, until she'd found this idyllic spot.

Now, in spite of the mosquitoes buzzing hungrily around her ears and ankles, she sat in silence, listening to the sounds of the night.

Remembering the sound of Lucas playing the saxophone.

It was the song. That was what had made her cry. That was what had made her long for something she couldn't envision, couldn't grasp. It was a lovely song—sweet and full of a tender yearning. Willa longed to know the words to the tune that lingered in her head like a music box being wound over and over. She also longed for answers to her confusing questions.

"Child, what are you doing out here all by yourself?"

Whirling, Willa was surprised to find Hilda Dorsette making her way up the path to the gazebo, the doorknob tip of her trusty walking cane gleaming silver in the night.

Getting up to come and help her, Willa said, "Oh, Aunt Hilda, you startled me. I thought I really was alone out here in the dark."

Hilda gave her a penetrating look. "Would you prefer it that way?"

"No, not at all. In fact, I'd love some company," Willa admitted, surprising herself. Then she sniffed.

Aunt Hilda placed an aged hand on her arm. "Have you been crying?"

Willa waited as the older woman settled onto one of the cushioned box seats. Then she sank down across from Aunt Hilda. "I...yes...I was feeling sorry for myself, I guess."

"Then you were not alone, after all."

"What do you mean?" Willa asked, wiping her damp face.

"God was here with you, Willa."

Willa held her breath, then let out a tired sigh. "Then I hope He was listening."

"Oh, He was. You can be sure of that. The Lord is always in His garden. It's here that He walks with us and listens to us—just as the old song says."

Without thinking, Willa said, "Then maybe that was the song—the one Lucas was playing earlier on the saxophone."

Hilda nodded. "Yes, I heard my nephew playing. Decided to take a walk myself." Then she gave Willa another sharp-eyed stare. "The song moved you?"

"It did. It was so…pretty."

Aunt Hilda settled, adjusting a flowing silk floral scarf around her shoulders. "I know the song he played. It wasn't the one to which I was referring, but it is another favorite of mine," she said, one hand on her cane as she sat on the bench. "It's a fairly modern church hymn, written by William Gaither in 1971. It's called 'Something Beautiful.'"

Willa closed her eyes briefly, wondering why Lucas had picked that particular song to play tonight. And wondering why it had moved her to tears as she'd stood there in the shadows, watching him play.

Opening her eyes, she asked Aunt Hilda, "Could you tell me the words?"

Aunt Hilda nodded. "I could—it's all about how the Lord takes us when we are broken and makes something beautiful out of our life. But I think it would be better if you came to church Sunday, as my guest, to hear the words for yourself. I'll make a request to the choir director.''

''Church?'' Willa held the one word near her heart, felt it settle there with a gentle tugging. ''It's been so long—''

''Too long, perhaps?'' Aunt Hilda asked, her smile all serenity and light. ''It doesn't matter, you know. He welcomes all of us back with open arms.''

Willa lifted her head. ''Aunt Hilda, can I ask you something?''

''Of course, darling.''

''Would it be…wrong of me to begin praying to God now, after not having done it for so very long?''

''Prayer is never wrong, love. And besides, He's always with you, even when you're not completely with Him.''

Willa digested that, then shook her head. ''It just seems as if…well, now that I'm facing some unpleasant things in my future…it just seems almost foolish to turn to Him now. I never appreciated my blessings when things were going great for me. I just went about my life, thinking I had things under control.''

''And now, you're finding you're not in control at all?''

''Not even a little bit. And I'm so tired. Just so tired.''

Aunt Hilda held out a plump hand. ''Come here, child.''

Willa couldn't resist that invitation. She crossed

the small space between them, then settled next to Aunt Hilda on the rounded bench, tears brimming in her eyes.

Aunt Hilda took her into her arms, hugging her close. "Rest then. Rest here as long as you need. You're safe now. You've come home to the Father."

Willa couldn't speak. So instead, she wept. Gently, with little sound, but with deep, cleansing, purging tears of relief and restoration. If only her haughty, distant adoptive mother would have ever held her in her arms. If only she could have known her real mother. Could have. Would have. There were so many things she needed to know, so many things she needed to take care of. Urgent, frightening things.

But not tonight. Tonight, in spite of her growing feelings for Lucas and her determination to curtail those feelings, she felt safe and secure, as if she truly had returned home from a very long journey.

"I don't know what's wrong with me," she said into Aunt Hilda's lace collar. "I'm acting like a big baby."

Hilda chuckled, then patted Willa on the arm. "Not a baby, dear. A child. A child who needs desperately to be held and loved."

"How did you know?"

"Oh, me?" Hilda lifted Willa's head, then placed a warm hand on her wet cheek. "I'm not referring to me. Our Father is holding you now, darling. And He won't let go."

Willa closed her eyes. "Never?"

"Ever," Aunt Hilda told her.

"You seem so sure. How can you do that—let go and just believe?"

Hilda waved a hand in the air. "Look around us. This is my Father's garden. He created all of this. He created you and me. And because He loved us so much that He was willing to send His son to give us everlasting life, I have to trust that no matter what happens to me, good or bad, God will be there to comfort and sustain me."

Willa thought about her future. She might be facing some very uncomfortable, life-altering things. And what if the worst did happen? Who would she have to turn to? Who would she have to trust?

"It would be nice to know that kind of assurance and comfort, no matter what."

Hilda sat silent for a minute, then said, "All you have to do in order to receive those gifts, those assurances, is accept. Accept that God will see you through." Then she took Willa's hands in hers and smiled.

By the time Lucas found them there, they were laughing and talking like old friends. It burned him to no end that Willa seemed to be having a great time with his aunt while he suffered in silent misery. But he hid that unwarranted jealousy behind his usual carefree manner.

Leaning into the open gazebo with a flourish, he asked, "Now what are you two whispering about, out here in the dark?" Fanning at his ear, he added, "With nasty mosquitoes gnawing at your heads."

Aunt Hilda lifted up off the bench, her hand tightly

encircling Willa's. Willa stood, but Lucas noticed she looked different somehow. Almost…peaceful.

And she also looked as if she'd been crying.

"Lucas, Willa is coming to church with us Sunday," Aunt Hilda said, beaming.

Lucas whistled low, then shot his aunt a loving but quizzical look. Then he studied Willa's face. "She got to you, didn't she, *jolie fille?*"

But before Willa could answer, Aunt Hilda shook her head. "Not me. Apparently, it was you. You and your saxophone. She liked the song you played. It touched her." She held a hand to her heart. "It touched her here, Lucas."

Lucas shut up his whining and stared in amazement at Willa. She did seem different. "Is that true?"

Willa's eyes went wide. "Your music, Lucas… It was so beautiful, so perfect. I don't know… I just walked and walked and I wound up here and then Aunt Hilda found me—"

"And we had a good heart-to-heart talk," Aunt Hilda said, filling in the blanks. "A good soul talk."

"Le coeur a ses raisons," Lucas replied dryly, wondering why he couldn't have been the one to break Willa's code of silence.

"Yes," Aunt Hilda said, nodding, "the heart does indeed have its reasons. And humans also have reasons for not opening our hearts to the abundant love in front of us."

"Is this a quiz?" Lucas asked, frustration dripping like Spanish moss from each word, his gaze still on Willa.

She looked more at peace, but she also looked as if she didn't want to talk to him.

"No," Aunt Hilda replied, smug and proper. "But you might want to relax and figure things out for yourself. Everything comes to pass in God's own good time, Lucas."

He ran a hand through his tattered curls. "*Oui,* but I'm tired of waiting for that good time to come."

His aunt stepped forward on tiptoes to give him a kiss. Lucas bent to receive the show of affection, his eyes moving over Willa.

"I'm going to turn in now, children," Aunt Hilda told them. "This has been a good night. A very good night."

She was still chuckling as she went off down the path.

"Shouldn't you help her to the house?" Willa asked, her voice strangely quiet.

"She would refuse my help. She has her pride." He gave her a sideways glance. "Besides, she's walking on air from saving another lost soul."

"She *has* been a tremendous help to me," Willa replied, her head bent. "At least, she's made me see that with God's help, I might be able to come to some conclusions about my life."

Lucas couldn't be angry for that. "Then I'm happy for you."

Willa caught his hand in hers. "I want you to be— happy, that is."

Casse pas mon coeur. He didn't say the words out loud, but he wanted to. He wanted to tell her, Then don't break my heart.

He gave an eloquent shrug, then pulled his hand from hers. "I'm happy. Completely happy." For about three seconds, he stood there, a hand on his hip. Then he pivoted toward her. "That's not the truth. I'm not happy. I used to think I was. But that was last week, before I saw you standing in my gardens."

Willa held her head down. "See, I've already made you regret—"

He pulled her close then, needing answers, wondering how she could tell his aunt things she had yet to tell him. "I don't regret meeting you. I only regret that you can't trust me the way you seem to trust my dear aunt. I want you to share with me the things you just told her."

"I didn't tell her anything, Lucas."

"You didn't?"

"No. We talked…about God. About me." She stopped, sucked in a breath. "Something happened here. Something I can't explain."

And then she burst into tears and fell into his arms.

Chapter Eight

Lucas held Willa tightly to him, the sound of her sobs echoing like a siren's call throughout his heart. He'd lived with three women, so he knew the effect of tears on a man. They could bring down Goliath.

But right now, he felt more like David with the slingshot. Terrified, but determined.

"What's the matter, love?" he asked, hoping she wouldn't hear how his voice shook.

Willa pulled away, wiping tears from her face as she stared at him. "Your aunt is such a remarkable woman."

"Obviously," he said on a dry note. "Since she brought you to tears."

"She did," Willa admitted, smiling through her anguish. "But I'm not upset."

"Oh, really. You're crying like a child, but you're not upset?" Lucas scratched his head in wonder. "You're gonna have to explain this to me."

Willa tilted her head, then clasped her hands in

front of her. "Your aunt made me feel so much better about so many things. She wants me to know the Lord, Lucas."

He had to smile at that. Aunt Hilda was a fierce prayer warrior, a crusader for all that was good and right. It didn't surprise him one bit that she'd gently urged Willa to find her way home again. Aunt Hilda could pick a stray out of crowd a mile away. But she could also bring that stray into the fold with love and tenderness and open arms.

"Aunt Hilda is like an angel here on earth," he said, his voice low and reverent. "She certainly took me under her wing."

Willa reached out a hand to touch his cheek. "It must have been so awful. Coming here to this strange, new place. Knowing your parents were gone forever."

He closed his eyes, leaned into her warm hand. "It was tough, for true. But she made things so…soft-focused and steady. She never dwelled on the loss of my parents, but she was always willing to listen to us when we had questions or when we were frightened." He felt a shudder running down his spine. "Lorna had nightmares—has had them all of her life. And Lacey…she just built up this wall like a shield. She's buried it all so deeply, I don't know if she can ever really be healed."

"And what about you?" Willa asked, her fingers stroking his jawline.

"*Moi?*" He gave her a self-deprecating smile. "Well, we needed a black sheep, and I guess I fit the bill. I've acted out every rage and frustration I've ever had. In some ways, I guess I'm still acting.''

Willa inched closer to him, her hand going from his face to his hair. "I've been acting, too, Lucas. But tonight…it's as if all the shams and facades have broken away. Somehow, I know I'm going to find the strength to do what I have to do.''

He tugged her close, needing this intimacy, needing to understand all the turmoil she seemed to be holding so tightly inside. "And what is it that you have to do, *chère?*''

She took a deep breath. Then she held her head away so she could look into his eyes. Lucas saw the bright light shining in her face, but he also saw a tremendous fear. A trepidation.

"Tell me," he urged, his hands on her back. "Tell me.''

She gave a slight nod, then started talking. "Last week, during a routine self-examination, I found a small lump on my right breast.'' In a calm, steady voice, she told him, "Lucas, I…I might have breast cancer.''

He had to suck in a breath. The words rang inside his head like a death toll. Breast cancer. Breast cancer. Then the anger set in. The old, easy anger that he'd held on to for so long. The anger toward God, the creator, and God, the taker of life.

"No," he said, simply and deeply. "No. That can't be. I won't let it be.''

Willa ran a hand through his hair, touched her fingers to his neck. "I have to go to the doctor,'' she said, as if trying to comfort him. "I have to make sure."

The urgency of her situation tore through him. "You didn't do that already? Why haven't you done that already?"

She looked down. "My doctor in New York did a physical exam, then scheduled a mammogram. The mammogram showed a small lump about the size of a pea."

Lucas held up a hand to interrupt her. "Then what on earth are you doing here? Shouldn't you be in the hospital, getting some sort of treatments?"

She dropped her hands to her sides. "My doctor wanted to do a biopsy right away, but he told me I had several options. He gave me lots of pamphlets to read, suggested some books on the subject, even said I could take a few days to get a second opinion. So that's why I'm here. I just needed some time…to think about what this might mean."

Anger and dread made Lucas irrational. "I can tell you exactly what it might mean, if you don't hurry."

"You don't have to tell me that," she said, pulling out of his arms to turn away. "Believe me, it's all I've been thinking about, night and day. But my doctor did tell me that if it is cancer, we have a few weeks to get everything in order…if I have to have surgery." With her back to him, she continued. "You have to understand, I'm not one to rush into anything. I need time to think, to decide about my future. That's why I came down here. So I could get away from all the distractions and just rest and think. Then when those two photographers showed up, I thought they'd found out. I was afraid I'd have to go back to New York, after all. And that would mean further delays.''

"Then you have to go to a doctor while you're here.'' He grabbed her by the arm, urging her to turn and face him. "I'll take you myself. I mean it, Willa. We'll go to New Orleans. There's a clinic there that specializes in cancer treatment—one of the best in the country.''

"I know," she said. "That's the other part of the reason I'm here. Lorna suggested it, and my doctor reluctantly gave the okay. Lorna thought it would be more private, having it done down here, and she graciously offered to go to the doctor with me and let me recuperate here if need be. New York is a small town when it comes to big news.''

Lucas listened, his anger simmering slowly and softly. "So Lorna has known about this all along.''

Of course, Lorna knew. He'd seen it in her eyes tonight. And he remembered her many warnings regarding Willa's need for rest and quiet. Two things *he* certainly hadn't bothered giving her. But then, nobody had bothered to tell him the truth, either. "Why didn't anyone let me in on this?''

"Because I asked Lorna to keep it a secret,'' Willa explained. "I figured the less people involved, the better chance of this not being discovered. I haven't told my agent or anyone in New York. My parents don't even know.''

"Then why did you tell Lorna?''

Willa shrugged, pushed at her hair. "I don't know why I even called Lorna last week...out of the blue.

I just needed to talk to someone—someone I could trust. And I'd had her on my mind a lot lately, since I missed her wedding. So I just called, and before I knew it, I'd told her the whole thing. I really didn't want to be alone, but I also didn't want my parents to rush home. So Lorna suggested I come down here.''

''But she didn't suggest you get to a doctor as soon as possible?''

''Oh, she wanted me to go to a specialist right away. She even scheduled the appointment—it's tomorrow morning. She's going to go with me under the pretense of shopping in New Orleans. I know I shouldn't have waited, but I needed a few days. I just needed—'' She stopped, sucked in a sob. ''I guess I needed to have someone hold me and tell me it would be all right.''

''And Aunt Hilda did that tonight, not even knowing?''

''Oh, she knew,'' Willa said, a fist to her mouth. ''Somehow, she knew. And somehow, she did make me feel much better.''

He looked at her then, seeing for the first time the fragility she'd tried so hard to hide. She'd been walking around with this…this disease inside her, all alone and afraid, not knowing where to turn.

And yet she's come to the gardens. In spite of his stinging hurt at being outside her circle of trust, he was glad for that, at least. As long as he had her near, he could keep her safe. He and God.

''You're in a good place now,'' he told her.

"You're safe. And you can stay here as long as you need."

"Aunt Hilda told me the same thing," she said with a little smile. "I don't deserve all this attention. I don't deserve your kindness."

"You're wrong there," Lucas said. "You're sick, Willa. You need someone to help you right now. And we can do that for you."

"I'll never forget this," she said, her face pale in the moonlight, her eyes lifting to meet his.

Lucas wanted to hold her close, wanted to wrap her in a comforting embrace. And he wanted to protect her, fight for her, keep her safe. "Do you still need to be held?"

"Yes," she said, the word catching in her throat.

"Viens ici," he whispered as he pulled her into his arms. "Come here, love."

She came to him, courage and fear warring in her eyes.

Lucas pulled her onto the cushioned box seat, settling her against his chest as he stroked her hair and kissed the top of her head. "We'll get through this, Willa. I promise you. We'll get through this together, no matter the outcome—good or bad."

Lucas held her there in the garden, with the stars and moon over them and the fragrance of paradise surrounding them. And he willed it to be so.

"I'm going to New Orleans with her."

Lucas looked at his sisters, saw the concern and determination in their eyes. He met those looks with one of his own. He'd been up since dawn, first to get his crop-dusting assignment done, then to make arrangements with Tobbie to have a couple of the Babineaux kids watch over his animals at his place in the swamp while he was away. And he was in no mood to argue with his well-meaning sisters.

"But I told you, I'd planned on going," Lorna said, her arms across her chest in a defiant stance. "I've already made the appointment for today and rearranged my schedule."

It was early morning, and so far, they were the only ones up. The sun streaming in through the dining room windows looked deceptively lightweight. In a couple of hours, it would be burning hot. It suited Lucas's mood.

"Well, un-arrange your schedule. Now you can plan on not going," Lucas replied, his hands on his hips, his chin jutting out as he stared her down. "I told her last night, I'm going to see her through this. And I aim to keep that promise. Whether she wants me there or not."

Lacey touched a hand to his arm. "Do you understand what that might mean, Lucas? You going through this with Willa?"

Lucas jerked away from her hand and the pity in her eyes. "Of course I do. I stayed up half the night, on the Internet, reading about breast cancer. I know all about the statistics—she's too young for this to be happening. But I also know she has a very good chance of licking this thing if we stop delaying and get on with it."

Lacey looked at Lorna. Lucas saw the compassion and concern in their eyes. "I know what you're thinking. That I shouldn't get involved. That I might regret this. But I'm telling you now, I *am* involved." He ran a hand through hair he hadn't bothered to comb since taking a quick shower. "I have to do this. I have to."

Lorna finally sighed. "All right. But you stick with her. Be supportive, not all doom and gloom. She needs to stay positive."

"I am positive," he told her. "I'm going to see her through this."

Lorna pushed away from the antique sideboard, ready to serve breakfast to their few guests. "Okay. And remember, we can't discuss this with anyone. Willa doesn't want the press to find out anything about this."

"I can be discreet," Lucas said. "But since you told everyone around here but me, I guess you don't believe that."

"I only told Lacey and Aunt Hilda," Lorna retorted. "And that was only after Willa finally allowed me to schedule the appointment. The urgency of the situation didn't allow for very much discussion."

"And she told me because I badgered her," Lacey said.

"But she couldn't tell me."

Lucas stared at his sisters, wondering what other secrets they were keeping amongst themselves. Wondering if they'd ever trust him completely. Well, he hadn't given them many reasons to trust him, he knew. Especially since the night of the flood when he'd left Lorna abandoned and alone in the mansion, in the dark.

I tried to get back to you. I tried so hard.

And yet, he'd failed once again.

Well, if this was another test, he wasn't going to fail this time.

"I guess y'all decided I didn't need to know any of this—that I'd just brush it off and go on about my business, like the uncaring, uninvolved person I am."

"Don't go getting all defensive," Lacey countered. "This has been hard on all of us, and we just thought it best, exactly as Willa said, the less people involved the better." Then her gaze softened. "And…we knew you'd take it hard, Lucas."

"Yeah, well, you were right there. I'm taking it very hard. But I'm also taking it very seriously." Then he gave them both a long, measuring look. "How can I not get involved—Willa is too young, too lovely, inside and out, for this. Even if…even if I barely knew her, I'd feel strongly about that."

"But you do know her now," Lacey replied gently. "So we worried about that, too. We were just trying to protect you, Lucas. Spare you any undue heartache."

"How very noble of both of you."

"I'm sorry, but when all of this first happened, I didn't think it *would* involve you." Lorna tried to explain. "I had promised Willa complete discretion, but Lacey had to know, since I expected her to cover for me at the restaurant."

"And Aunt Hilda guessed that something was wrong, so we told her. We needed her prayers."

"But no one needed me," Lucas said, bitterness coloring each word. "No one thought my prayers would matter."

"Well, now Willa needs you," Lorna said, whispering as footsteps echoed up the hallway. "Remember that, instead of being angry at us, okay?"

It had been a very long time since Lucas had felt the need to be needed. The privilege carried a tremendous amount of responsibility, something he'd shunned for most of his adult life, for reasons that were buried deep inside his heart. No wonder his sisters doubted he could handle it. He'd pretty much glossed over any real responsibility, on an emotional level, at least. He wasn't even sure he was ready to deal with all this.

As long as he didn't think about what the outcome might be, he could hold on. He refused to think of the vibrant, beautiful woman who'd come into his life as someone who might be dying. He wouldn't allow that to happen.

Willa walked into the room, her blue eyes wide with fear and hope, her smile as lovely as ever. "I heard my ride to New Orleans was waiting for me here."

"That'd be me," Lucas said, remembering the feel of her in his arms last night.

She gave him a surprised look. "I told you, Lorna is going with me."

"Not anymore," he countered. "I'm going, and that's final."

He saw the anger flaring pink against her pale skin. "Oh, really? Well, maybe you've forgotten I'm used to taking care of myself. I only agreed to let Lorna go because she knows the city better than I do.''

''And I know it better than the lot of you,'' he replied. ''Everything's ready. It'll take about an hour to get to the city, and we have a quiet place to stay at Lacey's town house in the Garden District. It's very private.''

Giving him a resigned look, she said, ''Well, it does seem as if you've covered everything.'' Then she turned to Lacey. ''Thank you.''

''It belonged to Neil's family,'' Lacey explained with a delicate shrug. ''It was left to him...then to me.''

''We all stay there when we go into the city,'' Lorna said, her smile strained.

''You're all being so perky,'' Willa said, laughing softly. ''Please don't put on any shows for my sake. I'm fine. And honestly, I can do this by myself if Lorna can't come along.''

Lucas shook his head. ''It's not a matter of Lorna not being able to come. It's that I'm going in her place. Now would you relax and let us help you? I give you my word, I'll behave myself. But I'm going.''

Willa pursed her lips, lowered her head, then tapped her foot. ''Okay,'' she said finally. ''I give up. You can be my chauffeur I suppose, since you've halfway been my tour guide and bodyguard anyway.''

''There you go,'' Lucas said, relieved that she'd seen things his way.

"Are you sure?" Lorna asked. "I could still tag along."

"She'll be okay," Lucas told them. "Let's get some breakfast in her before we take off."

"I'm not hungry," Willa said.

"Nonsense." Lorna turned to the sideboard. "Something light. How about some freshly baked oatmeal bread and some of Aunt Hilda's blueberry jam?"

"Just one slice," Willa replied. Taking the cup of hot tea Lacey handed her, she sank down on a chair. "You've all been so sweet to me."

"We're behind you all the way," Lorna told her. "I told you the night we first talked on the phone, you don't have to go through this alone."

Willa nodded, took a small bite of the thick slice of soft brown bread Lorna had given her. "Aunt Hilda told me I was never alone at all."

"She would know," Lucas said, trying to muster a reassuring smile. Then he turned serious. "And she's right." He pointed up. "He's there. And we're here to make sure He hears our prayers for you."

"I don't know what to say."

"Don't say a word. Just eat," Lorna coaxed. Then she asked, "Do you want me to contact your parents?"

"No." The one word was said with raised brows and a hiss of breath. "They're halfway across the world. Let's wait and see...." Her voice trailed off as she looked at her plate.

"Okay," Lorna told her. "You just say the word, and I'll track them down."

"Thank you."

Lucas watched as Willa nibbled the bread. Unable to eat, he loaded up on Lorna's rich, strong coffee instead. "So…we'll go to the town house first, get settled in. Mimi, one of Rosie Lee's cousins who lives in New Orleans, will be there to help out. Then on to the clinic. Dr. Savoie comes highly recommended. He's well respected and he's handled hundreds of cases just like yours."

"He's the best," Lacey said. "And he put off a golfing holiday just so he could see you this morning."

"At my insistence," Lorna said, smiling. "He likes my cooking. But he would have done it anyway. He's very dedicated to his patients."

"I believe you," Willa replied, dropping what was left of her bread onto a century-old china plate. "But I'd still appreciate those prayers." She looked at Lucas. "I'm ready."

Lucas held out a hand to her. He wished he could say the same.

Aunt Hilda came into the room dressed in a tailored teal-colored business suit. Turning to Willa, she said, "I have an early breakfast meeting with the Garden Club, but I wanted to see you before you leave. And I wanted to remind you that I expect you to be in church Sunday—whatever news you find in New Orleans."

"Thank you," Willa said as she got up to hug Aunt Hilda. Then she stood back, her eyes moving over each of their faces. "You know, after I confided in Lorna, she told me to come down here. She told me you would take care of me. But I never dreamed...I never knew family could be like this. I'm overwhelmed.''

Lucas watched as she paused, fought for control. She was a cool, tall blonde who'd made her living on her looks. And he knew she was terrified of what might happen to change that. But right now, he didn't care about her looks or her career.

Right now, with very little makeup and an earnest look shading her blue eyes the color of morning mist over water, she was a beautiful human being, inside and out.

And she needed him.

She also needed his God, his Christ, to see her through this. He couldn't speak, so he took her hand in his.

Then, silent and firm, his sisters joined hands and reached for Aunt Hilda. She took Willa's other hand and joined with Lacey and Lorna. Lorna reached for her brother's other hand.

The circle was complete.

''Let's pray,'' Aunt Hilda said without preamble.

And so they did. Aunt Hilda asked God to watch over Willa in this time of need. She asked Him to bless her family, as He always had. And she accepted that His will be done, no matter the outcome.

Lucas opened his eyes, determined to make sure God's will matched his own. Determined to see Willa through this and to keep her by his side. Because he didn't think he could forgive God a second time. And unlike his dear aunt, he couldn't accept that it was God's will for Willa to suffer or die. So he took the burden on, willing and ready to fight till the finish.

Willing and ready to defy even God in order to save the woman with whom he'd fallen in love.

Chapter Nine

Willa turned from the open French doors to find Lucas standing in the kitchen with two cups of coffee. He'd been talkative on the drive into the city, showing her the sights along the way, pointing out historic markers and famous plantations along the Old River Road. They'd sped along in his open Jeep as if they were going on a summer excursion instead of to the doctor's office.

She didn't know why she'd agreed to let him, instead of Lorna, bring her to New Orleans. Well, maybe she did know, deep down inside. She enjoyed his company, in spite of the turmoil that had brought her to Bayou le Jardin, in spite of her fear of getting so emotionally attached to him. And she did trust him. Lucas made her feel safe and secure, even when he had her heart fluttering. She'd have to keep all this in perspective, concentrate on why she was here instead of thinking about a future she couldn't have with the darkly handsome man who'd come with her.

Plus, on a logical note, she reminded herself Lorna had so many obligations at the bed and breakfast, it was probably better that Lucas had taken over. He seemed to be able to arrange his schedule to pretty much suit himself. But he always got things done. She'd give him points for that, at least.

And she'd give him points for being so incredibly sweet and caring. It was reassuring to have someone with her, even if that someone had railroaded his way into this trip. And yet, she had to wonder what his motives were. Why had he come with her? Out of concern, out of compassion, or was he getting too close, too involved, already? That was something she had tried to avoid. But she hadn't fought very valiantly against being with Lucas. Now, she doubted the rationale of letting him do this. She couldn't bear to hurt him, but if things went the wrong way, she might wind up doing exactly that.

As they'd entered the city traffic, a light rain had started to fall, and Lucas had pulled over to close the Jeep's top. He'd been quiet after that.

He was still quiet…and watchful. It brought her such comfort to have him here. But it also scared her. She couldn't become too dependent on Lucas Dorsette's good graces, and she wouldn't let him get too close to her, wouldn't let him think there was something, some sort of happy ending for them. She refused to allow herself that luxury.

"Thank you," she said as she took the cup he offered her. The warmth penetrated her cold, numb hands. "I can't seem to stop shaking," she said as she looked out at the rain that poured down over the secluded courtyard of Lacey's charming town house. Putting her confusion and doubts aside, she tried to absorb the ambience of the setting.

Nestled between several bigger mansions and estates, the tiny apartment had once been part of a grand residence just off St. Charles Avenue. The main house, closer to the street, had been turned into apartments, but this particular cottage, which had once obviously been part of the carriage house, was centered in a lush, tropical garden at the back of the estate.

Lucas came to stand beside her. "Are you sure you're all right?"

She nodded, her eyes on the banana fronds that dripped water onto the tiled courtyard floor in a precise melody. Nearby, a bougainvillea vine clung to a white lattice trellis, its hot-pink blossoms turned thirstily toward the welcoming rain.

Trying to hide her disturbing thoughts, she said, "I'm fine, Lucas. You've been so nice to me."

He held up a hand. "Please don't thank me again. You can stop being polite. In fact, you can shout and throw things if it'll make you feel better."

Willa looked around, summoned a weak smile. "I'd hate to destroy Lacey's lovely home. I have a feeling some of these Victorian antiques would be hard to replace."

"They're just things," he told her. "But you're right. Lacey would probably pitch a good tizzy fit if we broke anything—not so much for the commercial or historical value, but because this place was so special to her and Neil. It was a wedding present from

Neil's parents. Lacey and he spent their honeymoon here. Of course, she rarely comes here anymore.''

Willa put her coffee cup down on the white tiled counter. The tiny two-storied cottage reminded her of a dollhouse. Everything was tidy and in place. There was plenty of food in the pantry and fresh daisies on the counter, thanks to Rosie Lee's capable cousin Mimi, who'd discreetly left them alone until dinnertime. "How long were they married?"

"About five years. They were very happy.''

"What a tragedy.'' Willa didn't want to think about everything Lacey had suffered. She didn't know if she could bear that kind of pain, that kind of loss.

Apparently, Lucas didn't want to dwell on it, either. She saw the dark sadness in his eyes, but he quickly replaced it with a veiled look. He took her hand in his. "Let's talk about things with *us*.''

"Lucas—''

"Don't say it,'' he told her as he pulled her close. "Don't tell me there isn't something happening between you and me.''

Wishing she'd never agreed to let him come, she shook her head. "We have to face the possibility—''

Holding her an arm's length away with one hand, he looked at his watch. "We've got an hour before we're due at the clinic. I think we need to talk— about *all* the possibilities.''

He tugged her through a set of doors into the sitting room, which also faced the courtyard. Pointing to a bright gold and red floral high-back sofa, he said, "Sit.''

Willa settled onto the sofa, then rubbed her hands across her bare arms.

"Still chilled?"

She nodded. But this chill wasn't coming from the cooling rain outside. She was shivering with a deeply embedded fear that she couldn't even begin to understand or explain.

Lucas grabbed a mint green chenille throw off a nearby white brocade wing chair then tucked it around her. "I could build a fire."

"In the middle of summer?" She shook her head. "This is fine. I just got cold from the rain."

"Do you want to go up and take a nice, hot bath? I'll run the water then leave you alone, I promise."

"No. I don't want anything, thank you."

What she wanted was for him to curl up next to her and hold her forever. What she wanted was to keep on denying that she might be ill, to pretend that she and Lucas were here on a holiday. And that they had a chance of being together someday.

"Tell me what I can do, Willa."

It sounded like a plea. She looked at him, her eyes locking with his. She saw vivid pain in his rich brown-black eyes. Saw her unspoken fears reflected in the mystery of his gaze.

"Lucas." She held out a hand to him.

He sat beside her, then pulled her into his arms. "I love holding you," he told her, his words whisper thin as they glided over her hair. "I think I could hold you forever."

His statement echoed her thoughts, making Willa wonder once again if some higher power was working to bring them together. She lay her head on his shoulder, savoring the warmth of his skin through the cotton button-up shirt, savoring the fresh, clean smell that spoke of the forest and the swamp and the wind. Giving in to this one indulgence, she refused to think past being in his arms.

"I heard your plane early this morning," she said, her words intimate and low. "I couldn't sleep. It was just at sunrise. I heard the roar of the engine and I knew it was you."

His arms tightened around her. "I had to finish the job on that soybean field. Then I did a flyby over the house. I was thinking of you."

"And I was thinking of you, too," she replied. "How can that be? How can we feel this way after only a few days?"

If he heard the fear in her question or her surprise at the admission, he didn't call her on it. She felt him shrug. "Can't explain it, love. Aunt Hilda would say it's fate. That God brought us together."

"I'm beginning to believe that," she admitted. "I needed...help getting through this. I needed the courage to face this. I couldn't have done it alone in New York. Knowing I can go back to Bayou le Jardin to wait this out—"

"And attend church, as Aunt Hilda reminded us this morning—"

"Yes, and attend church. It means so much to me, Lucas. Your family has been so wonderful. I just feel as if Bayou le Jardin is the right place to be now."

"I'm glad you feel that way, but what about your parents?"

She stared at him. "I told you—"

"Never mind what you told me. Why don't you want them to know?"

Willa looked at the soft blanket covering her lap. "I'm afraid...I'm afraid they'll be disappointed in me."

"Disappointed? That you might be sick? That you might have cancer? I don't get that, love."

No, she supposed he wouldn't, coming from a loving, faithful family. So she tried to explain.

"My adoptive parents have always demanded perfection. They had my life all mapped out from the day they picked me up from the hospital. I would be educated in the best private schools in New York, then I would attend an exclusive, expensive college, then I would marry a hand-picked up-and-coming lawyer or politician and settle down to charity work and children, just as I told you before. And I would one day inherit a lot of old money to go along with my new position."

He tweaked her nose with a finger. "Sounds a bit boring, don't you think?"

"That's exactly what I thought," she said, a wry smile playing at her lips. "Which is why I rebelled big time and took off on probably what has been the only impulsive whim I've ever had in my life, to that photo shoot. The whim turned into a serious opportunity, though, so after I thought about it, I decided to sign with a top agency.

"I think I did it to escape. I'd never done anything like that in my life, never gone against my parents' wishes. But it just felt so good to be free, to be out on my own. Before long, I became very much in demand and I forgot all about my obligations to become a proper society wife. I don't think my parents have ever really forgiven me. I just can't bring myself to run begging to them now.''

"But they'd have to understand. Willa, they wouldn't turn their backs on you at a time like this.''

She fell against the sofa, wrapped her arms around him again. ''No, they'd be concerned and worried. They'd also demand I come to New York for any treatment or surgery, though. They'd have to be in control, and I'm sorry, this is my body. It's just way too personal to have them hovering over me and trying to control me the way they did all my life.'' She sighed, gave him an imploring look. ''I don't mean to sound harsh or ungrateful, it's just that I can't take the condemnation and…fear I know I'd see in their eyes.''

Lucas pulled a hand through her hair. ''Then we won't worry them unless we have to.''

She sat silent for a few precious minutes. She wanted to remember being held, wanted to cherish each touch, each caress Lucas had to offer. It could all change so soon. But she also needed to do one more thing before she gave in to this possible disease.

"Lucas, after we see the doctor, regardless of the outcome of the biopsy, I want to go and see my birth mother.''

He sat up, surprise evident on his face. "Are you sure?"

"Yes. If they find—if the doctor tells me I have to have surgery, I will do whatever it takes to survive. But first, I have to know. I have to find her and understand why she gave me up."

Lucas grabbed both her hands in his. "But not now. Willa, you can't put this off any longer. Dr. Savoie doesn't mess around. If he does a biopsy and finds something, then he'll want to go ahead and perform surgery."

"I understand that. That's why I want to go soon, after we're finished here tomorrow. I know where she lives, and I can go there and back overnight. Then I'll have a few days to rest for the surgery next week—if surgery is needed."

Lucas jumped up, then turned to stare at her. "Do you know the risk of stalling? Do you understand what could happen to you?"

Anger was her only defense against the passion in his words. "I understand completely. I've read all the information, talked to my doctor in New York and confirmed it with Dr. Savoie. Having breast cancer is serious. I know that. But I also know that doctors don't rush into doing radical surgery these days the way they used to. They've learned it's better to give women time to cope with this, time to make decisions and get things settled, just in case. Which is why I have to find my birth mother."

"You can't keep going like this, Willa. You've already waited too long as it is."

Throwing the cover off, she got up to face him. "Look, I just found the lump last week. I went to the doctor, but after he confirmed my fears, I panicked. That's when I canceled doing the runway show and that's when I called Lorna. It's only been a few days. If I do have to have some sort of radial surgery, I'll have to make preparations anyway. It won't be scheduled right away. I have time to do this, Lucas."

His dark brows shot up. "Make that *we,* suga'. Wherever you go, I'm going with you."

"No," she said, shaking her head. "I don't want you to do that. I need to do this one thing on my own."

"You plan on going way back up north to see your birth mother after having a biopsy?"

"Yes, that's exactly what I'm planning. And I was really hoping you'd understand and support me in this."

"I would have understood maybe before—before you told me everything." He stopped, gave her a long, searching look. "Or *have* you told me everything? Is there anything else I need to know, love, 'cause I'm not good at surprises."

Willa pulled away, then moved to the French doors. "I shouldn't have involved you in any of this. I tried to keep it quiet, tried to focus on getting to a doctor. It's only a matter of time before the tabloids find out about this—that's how they operate, slinking around until they get some tidbit of information. I didn't want to put your family in an awkward position—''

He was there beside her, pulling her around. "Hush. I've been in worse jams, believe me. I can handle reporters or anybody else who tries to get to you. What I can't deal with is not knowing the whole story. I need to know the truth, Willa.''

"Even if that truth turns out to be the worst possible scenario?''

"Even then.''

She gave him a wry smile. "You'll come to my rescue, protect me, help me, even if I have to go through the very worst?''

"Yes.''

It was a simple word, but its meaning wasn't lost on either of them.

She shook her head. "Maybe…maybe I should have stayed in New York. That probably would have been for the best. That's the only real truth I know.''

She saw the anger flaring like dark, churning waters in his eyes. "Right. Just like delaying treatment to come here was for the best. Just like trying to keep this a secret was for the best. Just like not trusting me was for the best—''

"I do trust you,'' she said, hurt by his condemning attitude. "Lucas, you have to understand—I'm not used to this. I wasn't raised to be open and frank. An O'Connor never shows any sign of weakness. That means no emotion, no loss of control. We walk proud and hold up our heads. We have an image to maintain, an impeccable reputation to live up to. We don't trust easily.''

In a move that left her head spinning, he pulled her close. She watched as the anger drained from his face, leaving his expression raw and wounded. ''I don't exactly inspire the trust of others,'' he said, holding her arms, his dark eyes filled with pain. ''But I'm asking you to give me a try. And I'll admit— I've never been through anything like this. I've had a sheltered, easy life since coming to Bayou le Jardin. Aunt Hilda used to tell us that we'd all already been tested enough, by the death of our parents. But then, she'd also remind us that life isn't always fair and that there might come a day when we'd be tested even more.''

Tugging her close, he added, ''I think this is one of those days, Willa. I think this is probably what my whole life has been building to. And I refuse to run from this, I refuse. You can't push me away that easily, regardless of what you might believe about me deep down inside.''

''Oh, Lucas,'' she said, hoping to make him see. ''It's not *you* I'm worried about. It's just that… Aunt Hilda was right. Life isn't fair. And it wouldn't be fair to ask you to—''

He put a finger to her mouth. ''Shh. We don't know anything at this point. You might not even have cancer. This just might be a big scare, all for nothing.''

Willa stood there, her gaze on his face, his lips. His finger moved over her mouth, then made a soft, sweet caress over her cheekbone. Then he brought his lips to hers in a searing seal, a bond that held them there while the rain fell outside.

Lucas lifted his mouth from hers. ''I'm with you, no matter what. Remember that.''

She closed her eyes, leaned her head on his shoulder and, even though she knew she'd have to leave him soon, she willed it to be so.

Chapter Ten

"How you feeling?"

Willa looked up after Lucas's question, watching as he maneuvered the Jeep inside the big garage at Bayou le Jardin. "Sore, and a bit tired, I guess."

She couldn't say more than that. The biopsy had gone well enough, if you considered having a large needle inserted in your body to draw out tissue as a fun event. Now they had to wait for Dr. Savoie's call. Willa had to wait at least twenty-four hours to see if her life was about to change forever.

Lucas took her hand in his. "Remember, Dr. Savoie said at age twenty-seven, your chances of having cancer are about one in twenty thousand."

"He also said the lump was very small," she added, glad Lucas had insisted on going into the doctor's office with her.

"Yep, less than a square centimeter." Lucas kept his hand on hers, and he kept on smiling. "And he did say it's good that you found it in time. You might

not have to have chemotherapy—just a few weeks of
radiation.''

His voice was both smooth and grainy, much like
the winding country road they had just traveled.
Willa knew Lucas was trying to reassure her, but the
discomfort radiating through her system only served
as a reminder that in the city, a pathologist could be
examining tissue from her body right now. Right
now.

She glanced over in time to catch Lucas watching
her. He quickly looked away, but she didn't miss the
worry in his eyes.

''Maybe we should have stayed another night in
New Orleans,'' he said. ''Mimi was willing to chaperon us a few more days. And I'm not sure what
she's going to do with all those ice packs she made
for you. Throw a party, I reckon.''

Willa had to smile at that endearing statement.
Mimi Babineaux was a bright, funny woman about
the same age as Willa. Obviously she'd been hand-
picked by Hilda Dorsette to watch out for her
nephew and his houseguest. Mimi had done a good
job, cooking up a storm for Lucas, hovering over
Willa after she'd been instructed by Dr. Savoie not
to eat anything before the biopsy, then fussing like a
mother hen when they'd returned from the clinic.

Lucas had insisted Willa go straight to bed with
an ice pack on her incision, and Mimi had made sure
the cold pack was comfortable, then she'd disappeared discreetly when she sensed Lucas and Willa
wanted to be alone.

Lucas had stayed right there, sitting in a chair by

the window while Willa slept, getting fresh ice packs when she gave the slightest hint of pain.

Willa marveled at him. He'd been so attentive, so tender. But she had to wonder—this was probably the strangest trip he'd ever taken to New Orleans. Not much chance to explore the lovely old city. Not much chance of exploring anything. Period.

"Does your aunt always provide chaperons when you take women to New Orleans?"

"I've never taken anyone else to Lacey's little retreat," he said, his dark eyes holding hers as they sat there in the quiet.

"I'm honored, then," she replied, her heartbeat accelerating much too fast. "And you've been a perfectly respectable housemate. I doubt we even needed Mimi supervising us."

He grinned then. "My good aunt probably thought I was going to spirit you away to do immoral things."

"Then she obviously doesn't know you at all."

He quirked a dark brow. "Must be losing my touch. You see, I've got everyone around here convinced I'm a bad seed. You won't tell them the truth, now, will you, love?"

Willa opened the passenger side door, grimacing with pain. Even though Lucas hopped out of the Jeep, she didn't wait for him to come around and help her out of the vehicle. She still had some pride. Standing to meet him, she asked, "The truth being that you didn't even once try to take advantage of me?"

He held the door, then leaned close. "Believe me,

the thought did cross my mind, but I do have some scruples. I respect you too much to pressure you into anything you aren't ready for—especially when you're wearing an ice pack.''

She had to laugh in spite of her discomfort. ''We weren't exactly in New Orleans for a romantic interlude, were we?''

He gave her a completely serious look, a look that tore through her heart and caused her much more pain than the incision the doctor had made. ''No, but I wouldn't have missed a minute of it. And I'd be a real cad if I tried anything crazy at a time like this.''

''Not to mention that Aunt Hilda would probably string you up by your sorry hide?''

''Ah, there is that minor detail. A man has to remember what he's been taught all his life. I know right from wrong.''

Willa stood, favoring her bandaged side while she balanced her weight by holding onto the door and Lucas's hand. ''Then why do you let people think the worst of you?''

Lucas shook his head, leaned close. ''Less explaining to do that way, I suppose.''

Willa touched her hand to a lock of curling hair at the nape of his neck. ''And less questions to answer? Less expectations to live up to?''

''You do know me,'' he said, a trace of awe and admiration in his words. Then he grabbed the hand she still held to his hair, taking it in his to hold it to his chest. ''Willa, are you sure you're okay? You look pale.''

Willa saw the sincere worry in his eyes—eyes that

reminded her of rich, dark chocolate. He'd promised her he could handle this, even the worst. But if the worst did happen, could she handle seeing that look in his eyes each time they were together? It would change to pity, and finally resentment. She wasn't ready to deal with that.

So she told him as much of the truth as she could allow. "I'm nervous, worried, but hopeful. And in some pain. But...I'm glad we came back here to wait for Dr. Savoie's call. I feel safe here."

"You are safe here," he told her, gently pulling her into his arms. "For as long as you want to stay."

"That depends on what the doctor tells us," she replied. "And we've still got a while to go before we get the results."

"Tomorrow morning, at the latest," Lucas said.

She was glad he hadn't mentioned her trip to see her birth mother. They had agreed to stay away from that subject for now. One step at a time, Willa reasoned. But she was going, regardless of what the doctor told her.

Lucas obviously mistook her quietness as a sign of worry. He held her away, then leaned close. "Remember, whatever happens—I mean, if you do need surgery and you decide to let Dr. Savoie be the one to operate, you can come right back here to get well."

"Thank you," Willa said. She didn't tell him that if she had to have a radical mastectomy, it would be hard to face him again, let alone continue a budding relationship with him. She wouldn't think about that.

Wouldn't think past today and whatever word they got from the doctor.

Right now, she only wanted to be held by him. She wanted to feel safe again before she hopped on a plane and went to find her birth mother. That trip would take all the strength she had left.

"Take me to the house," she whispered.

"Whatever the lady wants," Lucas said, easily sweeping her up into his arms.

"I didn't mean that literally. I can walk," she said, a breathless surprise moving through her aching body.

"Not when I'm here to carry you," he replied, his gaze holding hers as he gently tucked her right arm against her midsection. Then he kissed her, a quick peck on the cheek. "And Willa, I am here to carry you. And so is Christ. Remember that, please?"

Willa couldn't speak. So she lay her head against the warmth of his shoulder as he carried her up the path to the mansion. She wanted to give in to the desire of letting Lucas pamper and spoil her. She wanted to give in to the growing need that flowed through her like warm water whenever she was with him.

But she couldn't give in completely. Because she knew some burdens were too hard to bear. Even for a strong, capable man such as Lucas Dorsette.

If she became dependent on him, on his tender mercies and his delicate touch, it would only bring both of them heartache down the road. She wouldn't give Lucas or herself any false hopes. She wouldn't hold him to any promises, either.

Willa had always carried herself. She'd never expected anyone else to take over that job. Man or God.

And yet, her heart overflowed with a comforting security as she saw the now familiar sight of the great mansion looming among the oak trees. Bayou le Jardin.

Home. For a few more hours—for this one night.

For a while, at least, she was safe, cradled here in God's garden, where Lucas and his family could surround her with faith and hope.

Much later, Lucas knocked on Willa's bedroom door.

"Come in," she called, knowing instinctively it would be him. In spite of her resolve to keep things on a reasonable keel, in spite of the urgency she felt to find her birth mother, she had been sitting in a chair by the French doors, waiting for sunset and... him.

He came through the door, wearing a smile that took her breath away, carrying a cluster of Cherokee roses. The shades of dusk surrounded him, pale pinks and soft, creamy yellows, while the trees outside cast delicate shadows over the cherry-wood tester bed and the Queen Anne highboy. In the sunset, the polished woods flared to life with a rich brilliance that looked like fire dancing at dark. But Lucas's eyes danced with a warmth that radiated through the entire room.

Willa didn't say anything. She just sat there, taking in the sight of him. He wore old jeans and a faded chambray shirt; his dark hair was wet and glimmering and unruly.

Then he walked across the room and on bended knee offered her the flowers he'd brought. The delicate cream-colored clusters were sprinkled with a fine sheen of evening dew.

Willa took the flowers and fell completely in love with Lucas Dorsette.

That realization caused her to draw in her breath, caused her to go stiff and cold inside, in spite of her joy. She couldn't acknowledge this newfound love, couldn't tell him how he made her feel. That wouldn't be fair, wouldn't be right. Lucas deserved so much more than she could give right now.

"Hi," he said, still on his knee at her feet. "How you feeling, *chère?*"

She swallowed the hot, raw emotion catching in her throat. The way he said that one word, that term of endearment, made her close her eyes so he wouldn't see the truth that was clearly there.

He reached a hand to her face. "Hey, are you all right?"

She nodded, opened her eyes to find him much too close. Fighting hard for control, she said, "I'm fine. The flowers are so beautiful. Did you steal them out of Aunt Hilda's garden?"

He grinned. "Why call a florist, when I have some of the best bouquets in the world right in my backyard?"

"Probably saves on courting costs," she said, trying to sound upbeat in spite of her skipping, tripping heartbeat.

The grin changed to something else. He grew serious, his eyes every bit as rich and luminous as the polished wood surrounding them. "I don't go a'courting very often. And I don't steal flowers for just any girl, you know."

She forced a smile. "I'm so honored, Mr. Dorsette. First, you show me your secret garden. Then you take me up in your airplane. Then we visit Lacey's lovely home in New Orleans. And now, flowers." She lifted a brow, tried to hide the tremble in her voice. "And you expect me to believe I'm the first? Next you'll be telling me I'm the first woman you've ever been through a biopsy with."

His dark eyes went dangerously still. "The first and only, on all accounts—if I have things my way."

Willa sank back in the Chippendale floral chair, determined to remain intact in spite of the powerful charms of Lucas Dorsette. She couldn't let him have his way this time. For his sake. She had to keep telling herself, this was for his sake.

"Lucas," she said, holding the flowers to her chest, "I think we should talk. I'm still planning on going to find my birth mother—"

He leaned forward, a finger on her lips hushing her, but he didn't speak. Instead, he reached up to pull her head down. Then he kissed her.

Willa tried to steel herself against the onslaught of that kiss. She could feel the waning sun's warmth on her skin, could smell the fresh aroma of the soap Lucas had used to bathe mixing with the delicate scent of the flower blossoms, could taste the minty freshness of his mouth on hers. With a sigh, she dropped the flowers onto her lap and pulled her hands through his damp, curling hair. And somewhere in the back of her mind, a hope sprang to life.

What if she didn't have cancer, after all?

What if there was a chance for Lucas and her?

But then the solid fear of what her future might hold flashed like a warning sign in her head. No. She couldn't give in, not yet. She couldn't let this go any further until she had all the answers to tomorrow, regarding both her real mother and her health.

Lucas lifted his head, then wrapped his hands around hers to bring them to his mouth. He kissed her fingers, then said, "What happened? About midway, I lost you there."

"I'm sorry," she whispered, her hands clinging to his as he knelt in front of her. "I'm not ready...."

"I understand," he replied. Then he let her go to stand up. "I'm the one who should be apologizing. You're tired and recovering from the biopsy, and here I am like some adolescent schoolboy, pining away at your feet." He ran a hand through his hair, then pivoted to stare at the dusk-kissed gardens. "I only came to take you to dinner. If you feel up to going downstairs to eat in the dining room with the family."

She swallowed the need to go to him. "Maybe I should stay in my room."

He turned, concern evident on his face. "Do you hurt? Should I get you some pain medicine, call the doctor?"

She waved a hand. "No. I'm doing okay. I slept most of the afternoon. I'm just not very hungry."

"Aunt Hilda says you should eat. She and Rosie

Lee cooked up some mean chilled vegetable soup—all right out of the gardens and seasoned to perfection with fresh herbs. Do you want me to bring you a bowl?''

She shook her head. ''You go on to dinner, Lucas. I'll come later and have a glass of tea, maybe.''

He tilted his head. ''You can dip your corn bread in the soup—good for you.''

She had to laugh at that. ''My proper mother would be appalled if I did that, I'm afraid.''

He leaned down, placed a hand on each arm of the chair, then winked at her. ''Hey, your mamma ain't here, suga'. And what she don't know won't hurt her.''

''I suppose you're right there.''

Which was exactly why Willa hadn't called her parents in the first place.

''Good.'' Pushing off the chair, he stood straight again. ''I'm going to the kitchen to get you some soup and corn bread. And a big glass of tea.''

''Lucas, you don't have to do that.''

He stood with his thumbs caught in the belt loops of his jeans. ''I don't mind one bit. I'll be back in a few minutes.''

''Well, go ahead and eat something yourself,'' she said, hoping that would detain him for a while. She needed time to think, to decide what to do next.

She'd already phoned Samuel Frye. That had been one tough conversation. The worry and concern in her dear agent's voice had only magnified the situation for Willa. But Samuel had been a trooper once he'd gotten over the shock.

"Just get yourself well, kid," he'd told her in a soft, fatherly voice. "I'll take care of everything here with the agency and anyone who asks questions."

And there would be questions. Lots of questions. Which was why Willa had to think this through, weigh all the options. Right now, those options looked pretty dismal.

Lucas must have sensed her turmoil. He touched a hand to her chin. "We'll hear tomorrow. Then you can decide one way or the other—about all the possibilities."

He didn't have to tell her what he meant by that statement. Willa knew Lucas was watching and waiting, too. Because whatever they heard from the doctor would change both their lives forever, one way or another.

In spite of the prayers surrounding her, in spite of her shallow hopes of hearing good news, Willa knew in her heart that something was terribly wrong. She already knew what she'd hear from the doctor tomorrow.

And she already knew that there were no possibilities for any happiness between her and Lucas.

Unable to let him see the tears springing to her eyes, Willa turned toward the open French doors leading to the second-floor gallery.

And that's when a camera's flash went off, temporarily blinding her. Crying in surprise, she put her hands to her face. "Oh, no. Not now."

Then she saw the blur of Lucas's big form as he hurried past her and shot onto the gallery.

When Willa stopped seeing spots and regained her

focus, she saw Lucas standing on the gallery, his hands on his hips as he looked down. "Someone just got a picture of you, Willa. He must have shimmied up what's left of that oak tree Mick had to cut up after the tornado. That's about the only way somebody could get to the second floor." With a grunt, he hurried away, calling in a loud, angry voice. "And when I get my hands on that *somebody,* he's going to pay dearly."

"Lucas, wait!"

Before Willa could get out of the chair, he was gone, apparently taking the same escape route as the intruder, down the side of the gallery then onto the jutting tree branches.

Willa watched, her heart ramming a warning against her chest as she listened for a confrontation. Outside, the dusk quickly turned to darkness.

Now the worst had happened. If that photographer had heard something, anything, about her illness, it would be all over the papers tomorrow. And she wasn't ready for that. She wasn't ready to face the world with the truth. Not yet.

Chapter Eleven

"She's coming with me," Lucas informed Lorna a few minutes later. "Tobbie managed to run that photographer off, but he'll be back. And he'll probably be asking questions—about New Orleans, about Willa going to the clinic."

"You mean, you think the press might know something?" Lorna asked, careful to keep her voice down.

They were in the parlor. Lacey was with Willa behind closed curtains and locked doors in Willa's bedroom.

Lucas nodded, frustrated with this turn of events. He'd come so close to gaining Willa's trust, to holding her here with him a while longer. But now she was determined to get away, to hide out somewhere else. Or worse, make the dangerous, unsure trek to find her birth mother while trying to throw off those aggravating snoops. But he had other plans.

"Tobbie said he spotted a man earlier, talking to

Mrs. Gilbert, but he just thought based on the way the man looked and acted that he was another guest. Then he recognized him tonight as he was running away. It was the same man he'd seen with Mrs. Gilbert earlier.'' He waved a hand in the air. ''I sent Tobbie to find her. As soon as I have some answers, some information to confirm my suspicions, I'm taking Willa to my cabin in the swamp.''

Before Lorna could argue with that, a very contrite Mrs. Gilbert came hurrying into the room, her floral patio dress flowing out in ruffles around her plump body. ''Lucas, Tobbie explained what happened. I would have never talked to that horrid man if I'd known he was a reporter or photographer or whatever he was. He seemed so nice, so friendly. He said he'd noticed Willa while he was touring the gardens—to take pictures of the roses and other flowers—said that was why he was here. Said he did still life and landscape calendars. He never mentioned that he wanted a picture of Willa, too.''

She stopped long enough to inhale a much-needed breath. ''I'm afraid I told him who she was and that she'd come down here to rest. I added that it sounded as if she could use a good rest, from what I'd heard.'' Frowning, she muttered almost to herself, ''And to think, he assured me he would keep everything I told him a secret. Well, I never.''

Lorna frowned, then let out a sigh. ''But, Mrs. Gilbert, you promised to be discreet.''

''And I was,'' the older woman said through trembling lips. ''I've hardly thought about Willa for the last couple of days. Dr. Gilbert took me on a tour of the neighboring plantations, one yesterday and another one today, and in this heat, too. But…that man who called himself Jim came along with us. Said he'd never been to Oak Alley or Felicity. Said he could use them both for one of his calendars.'' Lowering her head, she added, ''Oh, dear, now I don't know what all I might have said. He did have a lot of questions about Willa's being here, about her needing rest and all. But I don't think I told him anything damaging. Oh, I just can't think straight, I'm so upset.''

Seeing the woman's agitation, Lorna tried to calm her down. ''It's all right, Mrs. Gilbert. The man was obviously very crafty. He tricked all of us. What else did you say to him?''

Mrs. Gilbert held a hand to her heart, then blinked. ''We got to talking about New Orleans. I told him I was afraid to go there. He said he might drive down to get some more pictures. Then he said he thought he'd seen Lucas and Willa leaving yesterday morning, heard they were going into the city for some sight-seeing or something. He even joked about what a lucky man Lucas was, getting to show Willa O'Connor all the sights and such.''

''Did you confirm that we did indeed go to New Orleans?'' Lucas asked her, trying to keep the impatience and anger out of his voice.

''I didn't even know you'd gone,'' the woman admitted, batting her eyes at Lucas. ''But I did tell him that you and Willa seemed to be growing awfully close. You see, I thought it was just so sweet. Oh,

I'm very sorry. I hope Willa isn't too upset with me.''

"It's okay," Lucas said, taking Mrs. Gilbert by the arm to guide her toward her room. "The man was probably watching and waiting, no telling how long he's been lurking about. He would have easily had enough time to get back from the tour and drive into New Orleans late yesterday. But there is no way he could have found us there. He probably hung around until he knew we were back here, then he waited until dusk to sneak up to Willa's room.'' Giving Lorna a stone-faced look, he said to Mrs. Gilbert, "Thanks for being honest with us. I'll take you back to your room.''

"That's not necessary," Mrs. Gilbert said. "We were just about to go to bed, since we're so exhausted from this heat. Mr. Gilbert is probably already asleep, so I don't want you to wake him. I'll find my way back to my room.''

Lucas watched as she hurried away, her head down, her lips in a pout. Then he said to Lorna in a low voice, "I just wonder… What if that man were snooping around? What if he heard Willa and me talking the other night in the garden, or maybe he heard us discussing everything the morning we left? You know how they operate, Lorna.''

Lorna lifted her brows. "Yes, I know. But do you really think it's wise to take Willa into the swamp?''

"They can't get to her there. I'll take her to my cabin—just for tonight, so she can at least get a good night's rest. Then tomorrow morning, we'll be back here in time for the doctor's call.'' At her doubtful look, he added, "It's just to throw them off, make them think Willa has left. And now that Tobbie and Mick know what's going on, they can inform them that she has indeed left—which will be the truth, technically speaking."

"Take your phone and your pager," Lorna told him, a finger in his face. "And make sure they've both got full power."

"Of course," Lucas replied, irritation snapping through his reply. Was that his sister's subtle way of reminding him he couldn't always be dependable?

Mick came in from the gallery, his expression grim. "Well, buddy. I've got good news and I've got bad news."

Lucas let out a sigh. "What?"

"The bad news—they were camped out at the main gate. Tobbie and I found a van with two of them inside—one was our tree-climbing friend, all right. Before we could tell 'em to get lost, one of them asked me if I knew what was wrong with Willa O'Connor. Said he'd heard from one of the other guests that she was sick. You're right, Lucas. They're beginning to figure things out."

Lucas put a hand to his head, gripping a wad of hair. "So what's the good news?"

"We sent 'em packing, and we called the sheriff to make sure if they do try anything they'll regret it."

"Thanks," Lucas said. "But we can't expect the sheriff to put out a patrol around the clock. I'm going to get Willa and we're going into the swamp. If they try to follow us, we'll let the 'gators deal with 'em."

"She's not going to like this," Lorna said. "She's not used to being whisked away in the night."

"Isn't she?" Lucas asked, spinning to stare at his sister. "Isn't this exactly how she has to live all the time? Isn't this why she's so afraid to trust anyone?"

Mick shot his wife a warning look, then put a hand on Lucas's arm. "I think what Lorna's trying to say is that Willa is capable of dealing with things like this on her own. She might not like your interference."

Lucas stared at Mick, then shrugged. "Well, tough. She doesn't have much choice this time. And she doesn't need this right now."

"What's going on?" Willa asked from the hallway, her skin pale, her eyes wary as she glanced from one face to the other. But she guessed it before anyone could speak. "Oh, no. They know, don't they? Lucas, they've found out?"

He couldn't lie to her. "We think so, love." He pulled her into the room. "But look, I'm going to get you out of here."

She looked skeptical. "Oh, yeah. And how are you going to do that? The only way to get past reporters is to take an airplane away from them, and your plane is miles away at the hangar."

"I'm taking you to my cabin in the swamp," he said, his expression brooking no argument. "Now. Tonight."

Willa gave him an incredulous look. "The swamp? No. Absolutely not. I have to leave anyway, might as well be now. If someone could just get me to the airport in New Orleans?"

"No way," Lucas said. "They'd follow you there, Willa. They've been watching the house and they might know we went to the clinic. The swamp is the one place they can't bother you."

"And what about the doctor?" she asked, her eyes glittering with anger and apprehension.

"If you want, we'll give Dr. Savoie both your cell phone numbers, then he can call you at the cabin," Lorna told her in a quiet voice. "Lucas will bring you back once we know something."

"This is crazy," Willa replied, her gaze sweeping over Lucas. "I can deal with this. I'm used to dealing with reporters and paparazzi. And I don't expect you to just drop everything to constantly hold my hand, Lucas. It's not necessary. I'll figure out something, some way to get past them."

Mick shot a look at Lucas, as if to say *I told you so.*

Ignoring his brother-in-law, Lucas stepped close, holding her arm with his hand. "But you're in the middle of a health crisis, Willa," he said. "What if they're snooping around when you get the phone call? Do you really want them putting your picture on one of their sleazy rags or printing something about you that is so personal and private? If they get the slightest hint that something is wrong, they won't stop until they get the whole story. What if they interview a doctor or nurse or someone else who works at the clinic?"

Willa pulled away, turned her back to him. Lucas could see her pride in the way she held herself erect and rigid, in the way she held her arms tightly folded against her stomach. She didn't even like discussing this in front of Lorna and Mick. He wanted to help her, and the only way he knew how was to take her to a safe haven.

"Willa?"

"Let's go," she said, her face still turned away. "Let's just get out of here."

Lucas glanced at Lorna and Mick. The sympathy he saw on their faces brought him some comfort. But Willa didn't want sympathy. She wasn't ready for that yet.

"Call us if you hear anything," he told Lorna. "And if you can't get through, send someone to get us."

Willa gave Lorna a stubborn look. "Have Dr. Savoie call my cell phone number first, please."

Lucas didn't argue with that. The results were between Willa and her doctor, after all. No matter how much he wanted to be there when she heard.

"We will." Lorna went to Willa. "You'll be fine. Lucas will keep you safe. And they won't dare try to go into the bayou."

"Thank you," Willa said. Then she turned and hugged Lorna. "I'm so sorry I've brought all of this on your family."

"Don't be silly," Lorna said. "That's what family is for. We look after each other, protect each other."

Willa glanced up then. "But—"

"Shh," Lorna said. "Just go with Lucas. Try to stay positive. And get some rest. Things will look better in the morning."

Lucas could tell by the drawn look on Willa's face

that she didn't believe it. She turned to him. "I'll get a few things and then I'll be ready," she said, a new determination evident in her blue eyes.

Lucas hoped it was a determination to survive. He needed her to fight, not only for herself, but for his love, too. He refused to let her give up. Because he knew he never could.

"It's so dark," Willa told him about an hour later. She watched, fascinated, as he used a long pole instead of a paddle to ease the narrow boat he called a pirogue through the brackish, swirling waters of the bayou.

"Darker than a 'gator's belly," he said over his shoulder. "Did you put on some of that bug repellent Rosie Lee gave us?"

"Yes," she replied, fanning away mosquitoes and other flying creatures she didn't want to think about. "It smells good, like lemons."

"Made from lemon grass. Pest don't like that smell, suga'."

"Thank goodness."

Their voices drifted off in a lost echo, then the still swamp became silent again, except for the bullfrogs croaking, the katydids singing and the occasional splash of some nocturnal creature slithering off the bank and into the water.

Willa tried to stay calm, but the pirogue was so small and only a few inches over the water. She didn't dare reach her hand over the edge of the boat to see just how far the black water was from her fingers. She concentrated on her surroundings.

"These trees are incredible," she said in a whisper, her gaze scanning the moss-draped giants.

"Cypress," Lucas told her. "As old as time. We're around in the back of the bayou now—they call it *Rivière de Doute*—the River of Doubt. Few men venture here. But I do love it, especially just after the sun begins to set—at first dark."

"More like very dark," Willa said, her laughter brittle as she squinted at the gray and black shapes swirling by here and there on the nearby shore. She felt as if she were lost in a never-ending labyrinth. In spite of the cloying humidity, she couldn't help the shivers running up and down her spine.

Needing to keep a connection with him, she said, "I must have been crazy, letting you talk me into this. Bringing me to the middle of the swamp—it's like the end of the earth."

"That's why it's completely safe," Lucas said, his head down as he watched the black water moving away from the swift boat. "I won't let anything happen to you, I promise."

"I believe you," she said, a measure of reassurance easing her fears. It felt strange, allowing someone to take care of things. She didn't dare get used to it. "I've been all over the world, but I've never done anything like this before."

"You live in a different sort of jungle, I reckon."

She smiled into the darkness. "I've never considered it that way." But then, he always made her see things in a different light.

He turned the boat into an open channel where blue and purple water hyacinths spread out like a patterned quilt, shining in the silver-shot rays of a crescent moon.

Willa sucked in her breath. "Lucas, it's so beautiful."

"Beautiful but deceiving," he said. "These pretty petals and vines, they choke up the water."

She saw the flash of his wry smile, felt the tug of that smile all the way to her toes. She did feel safe with him, even in the middle of the unforgiving swamp. She watched him, following his dark silhouette as he carried them toward home. His home.

He belongs here, she told herself, a grain of doubt rubbing at her tired mind. How could I begin to pull him away from this? Even if I'm okay. Even if I'm cancer-free. Do I really have a chance with this man? Could I really expect him to sit around waiting on me to jet in for a few days here and there between assignments?

She looked at the lovely flowers flowing by the boat, seeing them for what they really were. As pretty as the hyacinth were, Willa knew enough to see that Lucas was right. They were overtaking the water, sapping the strength out of the wetlands and the marsh. A lovely danger. Beautiful but deceiving, just as Lucas had said.

Wasn't that what she was to Lucas?

On the surface, she presented a pretty picture. A fashion model with what the world termed a perfect face and figure. But underneath it all, she was a liability to him, especially if she was as sick as she felt inside. And if she gave in to the need to be with him, she might become just as cloying and overpowering as these mysterious flowers.

And he'd resent her for that.

So many obstacles stood between them. Willa did indeed feel lost in the wilderness. Then she looked at the moon hanging so close, she thought she could reach out and touch it.

Are You up there, God? Are You listening? Can You help me to make the right decision? Help me to put these silly notions of love out of my mind, help me to let Lucas go. I won't pull him away from his home. I won't force him to make that kind of choice. No matter what tomorrow brings. Help me, Lord.

She didn't even realize she had been praying until Lucas stopped the pirogue near a small wooden dock. "We're here, love. Time for *le lit de repos*."

A little repose. A little bit of rest.

How she needed just that. But Willa didn't think she'd get much sleep this night. Not with the man she'd fallen so completely in love with watching over her.

And knowing that come tomorrow she'd have to leave him, one way or another.

"Allo," a voice called from the darkened shore. Then Willa saw a flashlight moving through the gray-tinged night.

"That's Royden," Lucas told her as he tied the boat then turned to help her out. "Just call him Roy Boy, everybody does. And don't flirt with him too much. He's only eighteen—the oldest of the Babineaux clan."

"Roy Boy." Willa had to laugh in spite of her mixed feelings about being here. "What's he doing—another chaperon sent by your aunt?"

"*Non.* We're on a mile-wide island out in the middle of the bayou. The Babineaux family lives just around the bend, so he watches the place for me when I'm along the front at the big house."

"Along the front?"

"Just swamp talk, *chère.* It means when I'm at Bayou le Jardin, I'm on the front end of the property. And this—this is in the back."

"Oh, you mean you're actually out in civilization when you leave this place?"

"*Oui.* Now you're catching on."

He helped her onto the dock, then took her red leather overnight bag. "How you feeling?"

"A little unsteady from that lovely swamp tour, but I'm okay."

In the next instant, a baying hound dog came running to greet them. Willa watched as the beautiful bluish-gray animal with small floppy ears jumped on Lucas, covering him completely to his chest.

"Is this another member of the Babineaux family?" she asked as the animal dropped down and begin sniffing at her linen pants, its white-gray eyes shining with a luminous glow in the fresh moonlight.

"He kinda belongs to the lot of us," Lucas replied. "But he thinks he's my *bébé.*" He fell to his knees to pet the huge animal, all the while cooing in French. "He's been banished from the mansion grounds—tends to chew up flower beds."

"What breed is he?" Willa asked, delighted with

the dog's doleful eyes and perky ears. She reached out a hand to touch him as he twisted away from Lucas to come sniffing at her pant leg again.

"A Catahoula hound—also known as a leopard. We call him Tulip."

"A hound named Tulip. Now that's different."

Roy Boy tugged the animal away from Willa, then grinned. "Somebody either lost him or let him go. Found him near dead underneath a tulip tree."

"Poor thing. So you named him Tulip. Makes perfect sense to me," Willa replied, reaching out to shake the young man's hand. "I'm Willa."

"Yes, ma'am, I know who you are, for true," the boy stammered. "Welcome to Bayou Fait."

She understood Lucas's warning to mind her flirting. The kid obviously knew a thing or two about supermodels.

"Thank you. And I probably don't want to know how this place got its name."

Roy Boy was only too happy to fill her in. "A trapper got lost in here over two hundred years ago. When dey found him he said dis was the place where a man would meet his fate, good or bad. He'd done gone 'bout half mad and refused to leave. Lived right up dere on dat hill for round fifty years."

Willa stared at the dark-haired boy, then turned to look at the hill he pointed toward. Tulip whimpered, then took off toward that very hill.

And the cabin.

It sat there, squatting in the dark night, all cypress planks and porches from what she could see from the flowing yellow lights illuminating it. "Did he live in that particular house?"

"Non," Roy Boy said as Lucas guided her toward the tiny square cabin. "His old shack fell slap apart, but Lucas, he built dis one to be exactly like da original. A trapper's cabin, for true."

A trapper's cabin. Willa could only shake her head. She was sick, unsure about her health or her future; she was recovering from a biopsy and she was standing deep in the Louisiana swamp with a man she'd only met a few days ago, and she was hopelessly in love with that man. The trapper. Well, he'd trapped her heart. But he wouldn't be able to keep her here. Her fate didn't lie in this beautiful, disturbing place with this beautiful, disturbing man.

Willa had to keep telling herself that.

As if sensing her hesitation, Lucas pulled her close before they started up the wide plank steps. "You know, suga', the Cajuns have a saying—'Today is gone, tomorrow come another day.' It's gonna be all right, Willa. Tomorrow will come, for both of us."

She looked at him, touched a hand to his face. "Yes, it will. And soon, I'll have to go back to that other world, back along the front as you call it. That's something we have to face, Lucas."

"But not tonight, love," he said, his dark eyes brimming with as many aged secrets and hidden treasures as his beloved bayou. "We have a few hours still, *oui?*"

Then he took her hand and led her up the steps, toward the welcoming lights of the cabin.

Chapter Twelve

"You didn't eat much dinner."

Lucas looked at Willa across the cypress plank table that filled the cabin's kitchen.

"I'm sorry," she said. "The jambalaya was very good, and it was so nice of Roy Boy to bring it. I just don't have much of an appetite tonight."

"Worried about those reporters?"

She looked at him, saw the reflection of his worry clearly in his dark eyes. "I guess so," she said. "I just wish…"

How could she tell him what she wished? How could she say what was in her heart, that she wished she'd met him long before a health scare had brought her to Louisiana? How could she tell him that she had fallen in love with him, in spite of her resolve, in spite of her pride, in spite of all her misgivings?

Willa couldn't believe she was in his cabin, lost in the middle of the wilds with him. The little house was primitive but efficient. It didn't have electricity, so they sat in the soft glow of kerosene lamps. Hurricane lamps, Lucas had called them. And candles. Candles sitting on every available surface, some scented, some merely effective. Lorna and Lacey's touch, he'd said with a sheepish grin.

But he hadn't let his sisters do much decorating. Only one picture graced the room. It was a pen-and-ink rendering of Bayou le Jardin, hanging in a rugged frame over the fireplace. A gift from his aunt Hilda, to remind him he always had a home when he got tired of his sanctuary here. Other than an old, worn brown leather couch, a few roughhewn cypress tables and one sturdy oak overloaded bookshelf that lined the wall opposite the fireplace, the place was sparse.

A trapper's cabin.

He had a pump at the sink for cooking and bathing water and an outdoor shower around back. And there was a bathroom of sorts—more of a water closet than a modern facility—and, thankfully, fresh water from an underground well—just no hot water. He used the old-fashioned potbellied stove to heat water and brew coffee, and he cooked on that or on the stone barbecue pit outside or by the fire in the sprawling fireplace that dominated one wall of the cypress room.

Outside, a wraparound porch, the back half screened, added a cozy touch. And the many rows of wind chimes hanging around the porch, made of every shape and size and object imaginable, lended a constantly sweet melody to the night. He obviously liked wind chimes, Willa thought, remembering the tiny bell chimes that had tinkled and swayed in the pagoda in his lost garden.

"Everything a man needs to survive," he'd explained to her as he'd given her the quick tour.

Or everything a man needed to hide.

And in the corner of the big square one-room cabin, a loft that was little more than a platform bed with cypress steps leading up to it. A loft with a big window, allowing a complete view of the bayou.

"So I can see the stars at night and the sunrise every morning." And the rain when it came pelting across the water and trees, he'd told her.

He reached a hand across the table, taking her fingers in his. "I like having you here, love. So tell me, what *do* you wish?"

She smiled, dropped her head. "I…I just wish the circumstances were better."

He dipped his head, slanted his dark brows. "We're together. That has to count for something."

"It does," she replied. "But Lucas—"

"I know what you're wishing. I know what you're worried about. We came together pretty fast and now you're wanting to step back, take some time and space to make sure we're not making a big mistake, right?"

She nodded, let out a long held breath. "Something like that. It's just that—"

"It's just that you might be facing major surgery and a long recovery and you're tired and scared and you don't want me to get too involved, right?"

"Right again." She held tightly to his hand. "I don't want to mislead you, Lucas. I don't want…to hurt you."

"I'm tough, you know. I've been through worse."

The husky tremor in those words pulled at her like the water's lapping waves touching the bayou banks. But like the shore, she resisted.

"I understand that, and for that very reason, I don't want to give you any false expectations."

"My expectations have already been surpassed," he replied, his black eyes dancing in the glow of the lamplight. "You are like a dream come true."

"Don't say that," she replied. "I'm not going to put you through this. This isn't a dream, Lucas. This is real. I'm real and I'm not as perfect as the pictures you've seen in the magazines. That image is fake. And we have to face reality. I won't let you nurse me through this sickness. It could get worse, much worse."

"You don't know that for sure."

"I have to face it, though."

"We'll face it together."

"No," she said, pulling free to get up and pace around the room. "I don't want your help, Lucas. I don't want you to do this out of some sense of duty, or worse, because you feel sorry for me." Hunching her shoulders, she looked at the worn floorboards. "I couldn't bear to have you see me if—"

She couldn't finish the thought, couldn't look past getting through this one hour at a time. Suddenly, the possibility of losing her career seemed small and insignificant compared to the dread and pity she might see in his eyes. And the repulsion.

He pushed his chair away from the table, scraping it across the planked floor. She didn't turn to face him, but she could hear the anger and the agony in his words.

"What I see is very clear. And I don't care about…the other, except for you to be healthy again. What I'm feeling for you is not pity or duty, *chère*. I'm falling for you."

She whirled, caught between elation and dejection. "You can't. You have to understand—"

He was in front of her, his hands touching her bare arms, his eyes holding hers. "Listen to me, Willa. It's too late to warn me. I fell for you the day I first saw you. That won't change now, no matter what happens."

She looked at him, saw the sincerity in the dark, flowing depths of his eyes. This man—this man was like no other she'd ever been around. Could it be possible that he really did see beyond the glamorous image, the carefully orchestrated exterior that had brought her fame and fortune, to the lonely, confused woman inside? Could he see that she needed him? That she'd been waiting for him all her life? Could he see that with him and his family she'd found the very thing for which she'd searched the world?

It was all right in front of her, at last. A home, a wonderful man, a life full of faith and hope and love, all those things the Bible talked about. Things she'd pushed to the back of her mind, things she'd never considered for herself. Always, she'd been too busy, too preoccupied with her image, with her career, with making it out there on her own. She'd been in charge, but she'd never really been in control.

And she surely wasn't in control right now, or

she'd be heading out the door instead of seriously considering falling into his arms and declaring how much she loved him.

Lucas must have sensed her confusion. He seized upon her silence, pulled her into his arms, kissed her long and hard. "Willa," he said, whispering her name on a sweet breath. "Willa, I *am* involved. Let me help you, love."

She looked at him, saw it all there in his face, in his eyes. So close. She caressed his face with her hands, savoring the roughness of his beard stubble, savoring the warmth of his skin. "You don't understand. I'm not used to asking for help or accepting help. I can't let you do this, Lucas. It's all too risky."

"Take a risk."

He kissed her again, then held her in his arms, with the candles flickering all around them. Outside, the dancing chimes picked up their tempo as the wind picked up speed. In the distance, thunder boomed like a warning bell.

"A storm's coming," he said into her hair. Then he pulled his hands through the blond waves, tugging them free of the silver filigree clasp she'd used to hold her hair off her face. It fell around her shoulders, down her back.

"Like spun gold," he said, his hands combing the thick, tangled tresses. He lifted a few strands to his face. "And the scent of honeysuckle and lilies."

A streak of lightning hissed through the night.

And in that flash of light, Willa saw his eyes, felt the power, the pull of attraction that had been bubbling around them since the day they'd met.

He repeated the statement, the plea. "Take a risk."

She wanted to do just that. A lot could happen here tonight. She was an adult; she knew how things progressed between a man and a woman. And yet, she also knew Lucas Dorsette. Maybe she'd known of him since she'd come into this world. He would never do anything to dishonor her. He would do what he believed to be morally right, based on the principles and values his aunt had taught him.

Based on his own beautiful character.

Lucas wanted more than a physical relationship. He wanted a full and total commitment. And right now, as much as she felt the joy of loving him, that kind of commitment frightened her. Because she might not be strong enough to survive the cancer. And that meant she'd lose him—and worse, he'd be left alone yet again.

"I'm not ready," she finally said, her voice cracking with the pain of denial. "Not yet. There are too many questions, too many things I have to work through. Please, Lucas, I'm asking you to be patient with me. To let me do this my way."

He stepped back, let go of a ragged breath. "So that means you'll leave here once you have the news from the doctor, good or bad. You'll go to see your birth mother. And then what?"

"I don't know," she admitted. "It's all so unsettled, so unpredictable. But I have to face facts. I have to get back to work, go on with my life. If I need to have surgery, then I'll have to make arrangements, make some long-term plans."

"Which won't include me, obviously." He turned,

listening to the approaching thunder. "Have you even thought about the positive side of things? Maybe we'll hear good news in the morning. Maybe the way will be clear for us—for a future together."

Willa shuddered in spite of the hot summer night. In a flash of clarity as brilliant as the lightning dancing angrily across the swamp, she at last saw what she was so afraid of, what she feared the most. She *was* worried about having a dreaded disease and the possibility of having her body cut up; those things certainly scared her. But, deep down inside, she was even more terrified of giving herself over to another human being. She was afraid to let go and love.

Wasn't that why she'd been running for so long? She'd run from her parents' misguided control and devotion, but she'd learned so very well from their emotional detachment. Willa had never learned how to deal with any kind of emotional intimacy and, because of that, she'd run from any kind of faith commitment. And now she wanted nothing more than to run away from what Lucas was offering her. Because she was so afraid she'd fail.

The revelation of what she was thinking and feeling left her shaken and drained. And silent.

Her silence was broken by another jagged streak of lightning and the almost frenzied ringing of the chimes as they tossed in the wind. But the message was clear.

Lucas didn't turn. "I see," he said with a sigh and a shrug. "What a complete fool I've been. All this time, I thought you were holding back because of the cancer thing. But that's not it at all, is it, love?" Then he whirled to glare at her. "You're just using that as a horribly convenient excuse, aren't you, Willa?"

Shocked, she took a step away from him. "What a terrible thing to say."

His eyes, so beautiful, so dark and mysterious, held a crystal-clear acknowledgment. "The truth is sometimes hard to swallow."

"You're wrong," she said, waving a hand in the air. "And you're the one who's not willing to face the truth."

"Oh, want to clue me in, then?"

"Yes. I'll be glad to do just that. Look, two weeks ago, my life was great. I was content in my work, I was happy. I had more money than I could ever use and I could travel anywhere in the world whenever the mood hit me. I could buy anything my heart desired. Then two things happened—I found out where my birth mother lived, and I found a lump on my breast."

She shifted, collapsed on one of the kitchen chairs. "My whole world, my life did a complete turn. Everything began spinning by so fast, I had to stop and catch my breath. I don't know why I called Lorna. I don't know why I came here. I just know that I needed to get away from that spinning world."

"You had to run," he said, accusation and understanding colliding in the statement.

"Yes, okay! I ran away. I wanted to hide out— deny that my carefully controlled existence had suddenly whirled out of control." Then she laughed, brittle and sharp. "Crazy me—I thought I'd find some sort of peace in the wilds of Louisiana."

"But you found me instead. I guess I put a definite kink in your armor."

Pushing hair off her face, she nodded. "Well, you've certainly broken through some of that armor. But I'm still spinning, still dizzy and sick with doubt and worry. You have to understand that. I have to find my balance again."

"So you'll just push me away?"

"I don't have any choice."

"But what about the other night? What about your talk in the garden with Aunt Hilda? What about how my song moved you to tears of joy? You seemed pretty steady that night. You…you *were* almost joyful."

"I was excited. That was no act. Your aunt helped me see things so differently, and I'll be forever grateful for that. She gave me the courage to tell you the truth and to go to the doctor the next day, to face the first hurdle. And I'm still trying to figure out that song."

"Well, thank goodness for small steps."

She hated the sarcasm in his words. Hated that she'd brought him to this.

"I do thank God—your God. And I've found some peace since coming here, in spite of the reporters, in spite of the biopsy and even in spite of— no, because of you. I want you to believe that, at least."

"Oh, I believe you. But He's your God, too. And until you can fully accept that, you will be afraid. You won't be able to make a commitment to me if you can't take a leap of faith."

She pounded a fist on the table. "Well, maybe I'm just not cut out to be a person of faith. Maybe I can't just accept things and go on, the way you have."

"What does that mean?"

The deadly calm in his question left her wishing she'd never spoken those words. "Nothing. I'm just trying to explain that I've got a lot to learn."

"And me, I've been through the wringer and yet I still hold out hope for a God I can't see or hear? Is that what you're saying? You make me sound like a poor sap who should be pitied."

"That's not what I'm saying. But Lucas, I know all about Africa and the death of your parents. Lorna told me everything. I'm not so sure I could have handled something so tragic. I admire how you and your sisters have held up."

He was angry. She could see it in the way he began pacing the long room like a cougar in a cage. "Yeah, we've held up just fine here in our narrow little world. We get knocked down but we just keep bouncing back. We get on with each day and we go to our little chapel each Sunday and ask the Lord for forgiveness and fortitude." Pivoting, he reached up to grip the massive cypress beam that formed a mantel over the fireplace. "I guess we do look pretty foolish to someone so worldly and sophisticated."

She slumped in the chair. "You're saying these things because I've hurt you. You know I don't see you like that at all, and you certainly can't believe that about yourself. You and your family have been so kind to me. For the first time in my life, I feel safe, protected, loved."

"Loved." He said the word, holding tight to the mantel as he stared into the empty black fireplace. "I do think I could love you, you know. And those words don't come easy for me. You talk about what I've been through. Well, you have no idea, no idea at all."

Willa dashed a hand across her face, the cold wetness of the tears she'd fought for so long breaking through her resistance. She couldn't bear to see him hurting like this. "Well, then, tell me. Talk to me. Help me understand how a person does keep on going."

He didn't speak. He held onto the shining, varnished wood as if it were a piece of flotsam lost in the middle of the river. Outside, a fierce clap of thunder heralded the driving rain.

And then she heard his voice over the sound of rain and chimes and thunder.

"It was a night like this one. Rain, so much rain. I won't go into the details, since you've already heard them. But let's just say the natives were restless that night. They wanted revenge, on something, someone. I didn't really understand their anger, since my parents had always tried to be kind to them."

Willa didn't dare move. She sat, her tears silent and steady.

"They killed my parents," he said on a long, shuddering breath. "Lacey witnessed it, heard my father's shouts to run, run away. So she took us and we hid underneath the round house. That's what we always called it—the round house. Little did we know it would become our refuge."

Willa bit her lip to keep from crying out, to keep from going to him. She sat still, waiting until he could speak again.

"Toward dawn, after the rain had stopped—when it was over—I ran for help. Lorna and Lacey didn't want me to leave them, didn't want me to go out there. But I knew, somehow I knew that I had to do this. I had to take care of my sisters. That was just the way things were." He shifted, held tighter to the cypress. Then he lay his head across one shoulder, as if to block out the painful memories. "My father always said, 'Take care of your sisters.' He'd say it when we went outside, whenever we went into the village, whenever we went down to the river's edge. 'You take care of your sisters, now, Lucas, you hear?'"

She saw the shudder of his dry sob. "I guess I've carried that voice with me every day of my life since then. I hear it in my dreams, run from it in my nightmares."

Willa got up, moved toward him, touched a hand on his arm. But he pushed her away.

"I didn't always."

"Always what?" she asked, her voice strained from the raw sobs she was trying so hard to hide, her hand going to her throat as she fought against pulling him into her arms.

"I didn't always take care of my sisters. I fought against that particular burden, that promise. Sometimes it just became too much. So I'd head off into the swamp. I'd hide out, shirk my duties."

"I can't see you ever shirking your duties. And

you've always been right there, Lucas. Lorna and Lacey love you, you have to know that.''

"Yeah, I know that. But you see, I don't take things like that very seriously. I like to play. I like to test God. I figure He tested me that night, so why not return the favor." He wiped his face on his T-shirt sleeve, lifted his head to the heavens. "I've stood on a boat with lightning sparking all around me and laughed in God's face. I laughed the night the tornado hit. I'm not proud of it, but I did. I just wanted to see what else He had in store for me. And then He brought the flood, and I was tested yet again. We almost lost Lorna because I didn't follow through.''

"But you saved a child," she reminded him, wishing she could take his tragic pain. "And Lorna is fine. She's happy now."

"Then why do I keep hearing my father's voice telling me to take care of my sisters?"

"I can't answer that except to tell you that you've done everything a brother could do. You have to let go sometime, don't you?"

She saw him sag, yet he still held tight to the mantel. "I want to let go, believe me. I'm just so very tired. I'm tiring of trying to understand. I'm tired of the memories. I'm tired of playing these endless games. Happy-go-lucky Lucas, always laughing, always having a high old time. I'm the life of the party, but it's getting mighty hard to keep laughing."

"But you survived. And you have such a strong, sure faith. You have to hang on to that."

"Oh, I'm hanging on, *chère*. Hanging by a sheer

thread. Aunt Hilda keeps that golden thread from breaking completely in two. The folks around here, they say, 'Dat Lucas, he gonna snap one day, for true.' But somehow, she always pulls me back in, saves me from myself.''

"She has absolute faith. I envy her that."

"Me, too," he admitted. "I'm such a failure, such a fake. I spout things to you about finding faith, about trusting in God, when I'm not sure I've ever really trusted Him myself."

This time, she did touch him, and this time, she didn't let him push her away. Wrapping her arms around his stomach, Willa leaned into his broad back. "Don't say that. You've taught me more about faith, more about God than I ever had with my parents' arrogant show of religion. Please, Lucas, you've got to stop punishing yourself this way. And please, don't let my doubts and shortcomings make you think you've failed me in any way."

"Haven't I, though?" he asked, his back stiff as he fought against her touch. "You refuse to consider a relationship with me. Not very good for my ego, love."

Glad he'd found a trace of his sense of humor again, she said, "Your ego will survive. I've heard the tales of you—you're a legend around these parts."

He wasn't amused at her feeble attempt to tease him. "Yeah, I'm a regular lady's man."

"You sure got my attention," she replied, burying her face against the warmth of his shirt.

In a move so swift she almost lost her balance, he

twisted, then caught her, his big hands on her wrists as she fell against him. His eyes held a fine mist of unshed tears and a darkness that scared her even while it tugged at her. "You see, that's the funny part. I've survived the worst a kid could see and I've taunted and teased God ever since. I've never taken anything seriously in my life. I've played at things— jobs, relationships, women." He let go of her wrists, then pulled his hands through her hair, forcing her head up. "And then you came along. And suddenly, I'm taking life very seriously. You talk about spinning out of control—*oui*, I know that feeling. *Vous avez saisi mon coeur.* You've taken my heart."

Willa cried as he held her there. "I didn't mean for this to happen. I tried to warn you."

He brushed a tear from her cheek, then kissed his wet fingers before touching them to her lips. "Too late. Much too late."

The rain came softly, falling on the shingled roof like tears from the clouds. The wind chimes settled to a gentle, soothing melody, a sweet song of the night. Lucas lifted her off her feet and into his arms. As he carried her up the broad steps to the loft, he whispered phrases to her in French. Phrases of love, phrases of hope.

Then he gently lay her on the bed. "Sleep now, *mon amour*. Rest. I promised you rest and peace. And when you're ready, I want to give you so much more."

He turned away, but not before she saw the sheen of tears cresting like black, raging waves in his eyes.

Willa lay there, her tears wetting his pillow as the

scent of spices and forest glades assaulted her. She wanted to give him more, too. So much more.

But first, she had to get her life in order. She had to get her life back.

She would do just that, no matter what came tomorrow. In spite of her fears, she made a promise to herself, to God and to Lucas.

I will return to you, Lucas. Somehow.

Chapter Thirteen

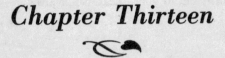

Willa woke to the sound of her cell phone ringing and a dog barking in the distance. Her overnight bag was sitting near the foot of the bed. Groggy and disoriented, she slipped down the bed to grab the bag and find the annoying phone.

Then memories washed over her with the same intensity as the morning sun shining across the rippling water outside the big window. She was in Lucas's cabin. Waiting to hear from Dr. Savoie.

But where was Lucas? He'd slept on the couch; she remembered that from her sleepless night of tossing and turning. She had seen him, his feet propped on a worn table, his hands crossed behind his head as he stared into the empty fireplace. She'd woken to find him bent over, his head against his clasped hands, almost as if he were deep in prayer. That had brought her some comfort, and finally the rain had ended. Toward dawn, Willa had gone into a deep, dreamless sleep. Now she wondered, had Lucas managed to get any sleep at all?

She saw him at about the same time she answered the phone. He was on the back side of the island yard with little Tobias. They were riding a big black horse with a smattering of white spots across its flanks and rump, Tulip nipping at the big animal's heels. Willa watched Lucas holding the beautiful little boy close in front of him on the big horse, her heart thumping in cadence with the hoofbeats of the magnificent prancing stallion.

"Hello?" she said into the phone, dreading the call.

"Willa, this is Dr. Savoie. Lorna Dorsette gave me your cell phone number. Can you hear me? The line is full of static."

"I can hear you," she answered, her eyes locked on the man who rode the horse with nothing more than a saddle blanket, rode the animal in jeans and an open shirt and old battered cowboy boots and an even more battered straw cowboy hat, a wry smile on his face. While she watched, Lucas bent his head low, saying something into the little boy's ear that made the child giggle.

"Willa, I'm afraid the biopsy proved our worst fears. The lump is malignant."

"I see," she said, her heart picking up its beat as she nervously clutched the phone. "What now?"

But she knew the answer to that particular question.

Now she would have to run again.

"Well, you do have some options. It's a small

lump—just under one point five centimeters. I think we might be able to save the breast by doing a lumpectomy. As I told you during our examination the other day, as long as the cancer hasn't spread to the lymph nodes, with aggressive treatment your chances of a full recovery are good."

"Good but not excellent? Not one hundred percent certain?"

"No one can ever be completely certain about cancer, Willa. But you have a chance. Based on all the tests, and again, based on the small size of the lump, I feel pretty good about things."

Willa swallowed, saw Lucas and little Tobias laughing as Tulip barked and chased horse and riders around the big, sloping yard. What a beautiful, tranquil picture they made out there among the glistening wet, towering cypress trees.

She closed her eyes to the beauty. Closed her eyes and refused to cry. "Dr. Savoie, I have some personal things I need to take care of before I make a decision. How long do I have?"

"I wouldn't hold off too long," the doctor said, his voice sounding distant and hollow. "But you could take a week or so. Would you like me to schedule the surgery here in New Orleans, or do you want your doctor in New York to do the procedure?"

Willa opened her eyes, thought about that. She felt completely comfortable with Dr. Savoie. He'd been compassionate and honest with her, and very thorough in explaining all the intricate details of breast cancer. And yet how could she stay here and have

the surgery so close to Lucas? He'd want to be there.
And he'd want to be a big part of her recovery.

She couldn't let that happen.

"Can I call you back?" she asked. "I have to go
to New York to arrange my schedule. I'll talk to my
doctor there and see what he thinks."

"Whatever you feel comfortable with," Dr. Savoie replied. "Of course, we'll be happy to send Dr.
Carlton your complete workup, all the tests and results, the mammograms, the X rays, all your current
records. And I'll call him to go over my recommen-
dations. I'm sure he'll agree that a lumpectomy is the
best choice, that is, if you agree to that."

"Thank you," Willa said. After assuring Dr. Savoie that she wouldn't delay things, she hung up the
phone, then sat cross-legged on the bed. For one long
minute, she wanted to call Lucas, to tell him what
she'd found out. To run into his arms and seek comfort and safety.

But she decided he didn't need to know right this
minute, and if she went into his arms she might not
have the courage to leave him.

She couldn't bring herself to walk down there and
tell him the truth. Not yet.

Somehow, she had to get to the mansion without
him knowing she'd found out the results. And then,
somehow, she had to leave. She would book a flight
to New York so she could find her birth mother. Only
then would she be ready for surgery.

And the future.

Lucas waved goodbye to Little Tobbie and sent
the rambunctious boy running up the lane to his

house. He turned to find Willa coming down the back steps, a cup of coffee in each hand, Tulip asking for attention around her feet. Filled with regrets he couldn't even begin to understand, he watched the way her long, loose hair flowed down her back, the way her baggy black linen clam digger pants and soft pink cotton T-shirt floated around her slender body. She'd slept in her clothes, but she looked as if she'd stepped right out of the pages of one of those famous uppity magazines.

If he ignored the dark circles underneath her blue eyes and the lines of fatigue around her rosy lips.

She called to him. "Where's little Tobbie?"

"Sent him on back home to his mamma. That boy does like to sneak off. Found him fishing clear on the other side of the bayou."

She nodded, stood looking at him with a hesitant expression, the cup of coffee held out like a peace offering.

"C'mon, Zephyr," he commanded the massive animal, "let's go see Miss Willa."

Zephyr snorted, pranced, neighed softly, then trotted to where Willa stood watching them. Tulip spied a wood duck off the shore and headed out in hot pursuit. Willa smiled at the hound's intense efforts, but Lucas saw the strain behind that smile.

"How ya doing, *mon coeur?*"

"I'm okay," she said, handing him the steaming mug of coffee. "I hope I made this strong enough for you."

He didn't need caffeine this morning. He only

needed to see her standing there. He imagined seeing her like this each and every morning for the rest of their lives.

Then he remembered why he'd brought her here. "Heard anything?"

She looked into her coffee mug, hesitated. "No." Then she glanced at the pawing horse. "Who's your friend?"

Lucas petted the stallion's long mane, then took a swig of coffee. "This is Zephyr. A big old Appaloosa baby that we loan out for breeding now and again."

She shot him a sideways glance. "You seem to like animals with spots."

He tipped the aged straw hat back, managed what he hoped was a rakish grin. "I never thought about it, but you're right. My dog and my horse kinda match, don't they?"

"You'd make a great fashion statement, that is, if anyone could ever keep the three of you together and still long enough to get a picture."

Bringing the hat low over his brow, he leaned his head down. "Ain't gonna happen. We've got restless blood in our veins."

She gave him a look that told him she agreed with him. "Just how many animals do you have here in this swamp menagerie, anyway?"

"This is about it, other than the natural swamp dwellers. Actually, the Babineaux clan takes care of them more than I do. They belong to me, but since I'm in and out, the family looks after them for me and generally spoils both the horse and the dog rotten."

"Why do you keep Zephyr here instead of at the mansion? Or let me guess—he likes to dig in the flower beds, too?"

He handed her the cup of coffee so he could dismount. Leaving Zephyr to graze on some nearby grass, he took the coffee then sat on the wide plank steps. "I had him stabled there when I first bought him, but he got downright lonely. That made him a tad skittish around the guests. Aunt Hilda was afraid he'd bolt and hurt somebody. So the kids begged me to bring him out to this place. He's been in heaven ever since. He's got about twenty acres to roam around on with the kids. They ride him, feed him, pamper him. And I know he's safe and well cared for when I can't be around. But this morning, I had a hankering to take a long ride around the property, get my thoughts in order." *Trying to get you out of my mind.*

"Will you take me for a ride?"

Surprised, Lucas looked at her, saw the hope and longing in her morning-glory eyes. That gave him some hope of his own. Maybe she'd thought about things, too. And maybe she had a new attitude this morning.

"Whatever the lady wants."

She pushed her hair off her face, her words as soft as a dove's wings fluttering on the morning air. "I want to ride with you on that horse."

"Are you sure? I mean, you're not too sore still?"

She looked into the distance. "I'm fine. Humor me, Lucas."

It was almost a plea. How could he refuse such a

soft-as-velvet request? How could he refuse another opportunity to hold her close. ''Of course.'' He whistled, bringing the stallion's ears up. ''C'mere, you big brute. The lady wants to meet you, up close and personal.''

A few minutes later, they headed down the dirt lane that led from Lucas's cabin to the Babineaux compound. The morning was sultry with heat, but a warm breeze pushed through the humidity. Lucas held Willa in front of him, taking in the scent of her long hair, taking in the feel of having her with him.

But something didn't seem right. She was tense and much too quiet. It gave him a sick feeling deep inside his gut. ''Are you sure you're okay?''

''I'm great,'' she said over her shoulder. ''This is wonderful. First an airplane, now a horse. You take my breath away, Mr. Dorsette.''

He brought the impatient Appaloosa to a halt underneath a great century-old magnolia tree. Then he leaned forward to nuzzle Willa's tempting neck. ''That's the intent.''

''It's working,'' she said, turning to face him as she brought a hand up and curled it around his head. Then she kissed him, a wistful, sweet gesture that said so much more than words. ''I'm going to miss you, Lucas.''

He looked at her, his heart as scattered as moss in the wind. ''Now look who's breathless. I can't breathe around you. And I can't imagine how I'm going to find air after you're gone.''

She touched her hand to his face. ''But you do understand I have to go. You do understand—''

"No, I don't," he said, his hand covering hers. "I thought about this over and over when I took Zephyr out just before dawn. You want this, Willa. I can see it, feel it, whenever we're together. Why are you fighting me?"

"Because I care about you."

"Hmph. You make it sound as if I'm a brother."

"Not a brother. A friend, someone who's helped me through some very rough spots."

"But someone who isn't allowed to take things any further?"

"Right now, no."

He kissed her again, just to prove her wrong. "When?" he asked, his lips grazing hers.

"I can't answer that."

He looked at her, saw the truth in her eyes. His heart started pumping a warning. "You heard from the doctor, didn't you?"

She pulled away. Turned. The tense silence spoke loud and clear. "Take me back, Lucas."

"Willa?"

"Don't make me do this. I don't want to lie to you. Just take me back to Bayou le Jardin. I have to leave. Today. I'm sorry I didn't tell you right away, but I just wanted a little more time with you."

He held the horse steady, then pulled Willa tightly against his chest. He could feel her heart beating right along with his, as fast as his. "It's bad news, isn't it, love?"

"I didn't want you to know," she whispered as she fell against him. "I thought I could get away without you knowing."

He swallowed, gripped her tightly. Then he leaned close, his lips touching her ear, his whisper like velvet. "Did you think you could keep this from me, Willa? Do you think you can stop me from caring?"

He felt the shudder of her sob. "I don't know. I just know that I have to do this my way. I need you to understand that, Lucas."

"So you'll run away again? You'll leave to go through this terrible thing all alone?"

"It's the only way."

"What about our future?"

She lifted out of his arms, strained to face him. "We might not have a future. Can't you see that?"

With a growl, Lucas lifted her body around so he could face her completely, then he pulled her into his arms. "And can't you see that we could have everything?"

She shook her head. "Dr. Savoie says there are no guarantees."

Holding her chin so she had to look into his eyes, Lucas asked, "Have there ever been?"

But he'd already lost this battle. He could feel it in the way she held her tears in check, in the way she refused to look at him. The silence stretched between them like an ever-widening river as he held her there. The stallion, sensing something was amiss, pranced and neighed. But Willa didn't answer the question.

And yet the sounds of life echoed all around them, in and out of the shadows of trees and water. In the lush woods, two blue jays fussed and played. Near the shoreline a fat, brown-haired nutria dashed toward a safe haven, and somewhere in the thicket, a mourning dove called for its mate.

Lucas's heart echoed that sad, cooing sound. He'd heard a dove's sweet song the day he'd taken Willa to his garden, and now it made him feel so very lonely. "Don't leave me," he said into her hair. "Let me go with you, at least."

She lifted her head, leaving a damp spot on his shirt. "Listen to me, Lucas. If I can find a way to beat this, I promise, I'll come back to you."

"You're bluffing," he replied. "You're just looking for an excuse to escape."

"Dying isn't an excuse. It's a reality."

"One you're willing to face all alone?"

She nodded. "Isn't that how we all die anyway? I mean, we go into the afterlife all alone, don't we? We leave loved ones behind, hurt and confused. I won't do that to you."

"Forget about me being hurt and confused! I'm already that. You don't have to be alone," he reminded her. "You have me, you have my family, your parents and you have God. That means you have more than an afterlife, you have eternal life. But you are never alone."

Wiping her eyes, she smiled. "I understand that now, and I'm beginning to believe, to feel stronger in my faith. But I won't make you suffer again, Lucas. Not on my account."

He gazed at her, at last seeing that she was walking away in order to spare him any further pain. "Don't be so noble, *chère*. There's a whole lot of living left here on earth before we meet our Maker.

And if I have things my way, you won't be going to the Pearly Gates for a very long time.''

"I have to be sure," she told him. "And I won't let you do anything you'll regret down the road."

"I told you it's too late for that."

"I'm going, Lucas," she said gently but firmly, her resolve obvious. "I've already called Lorna. She's making arrangements for a flight out of New Orleans later today. And if you won't take me back to the mansion, I'll get Roy Boy to do it."

Frustrated and angry that he'd once again been the last one to know the details of the very things that were sorely affecting his life and well-being and those of the woman he loved, Lucas reached for the reins and jerked the big animal into motion. "You want to leave, Willa? Okay. Fine. I get it. I'm tired of begging. But I won't be the one to take you back, and I won't watch you leave. I can't do that. Roy Boy knows the way. And obviously, you'll do just fine once you're back on solid ground."

Holding Willa steady, he put the horse into a fast trot and tried to forget that this might be the last time he'd ever hold her.

In a matter of minutes, they were at the cabin, and Lucas was pressing buttons on the cell phone. "Roy Boy, I need a favor. Can you bring a skiff around to take Willa back to Bayou le Jardin?"

Hanging up, he threw the offending phone across the room then turned to her. He hated the hurt, confused expression on her face, hated the fact that she needed him but refused to acknowledge that need, hated doing this to her. But this was the way she wanted it.

"Whatever the lady wants," he said. "You're on your own from here on out."

In his heart, he knew that wasn't the truth. Knew that he'd find a way to get to her. She had only to call, she had only to ask. But he refused to tell her that. He had some pride left, after all.

"I hope everything goes the way you want, Willa. And I hope you'll be...*en bonne santé*. Healthy, always."

Then he headed out the door, got on the stallion and galloped away.

"Lucas didn't bring you back?" Lorna asked Willa a couple of hours later. She'd hurried into Willa's room to let her know that the reporters had finally given up and left, after several strong suggestions from Tobbie, Mick and Mick's friend Josh. Not to mention the sheriff.

"No." Willa finished packing, then glanced around the bedroom. "He...he was angry with me."

Lorna threw up her hands in frustration. "Well, can you blame him? Willa, you don't need to go off and suffer in silence, you know. If you won't notify your parents, at least have the surgery in New Orleans, so you can be near us. You'll need someone to help you out for a few weeks."

"I'll be fine in New York. I'm going to go back to my parents' estate, where it's private and quiet. I'll have help there...and I'll hire a nurse."

"A nurse? That's ridiculous." Lorna stared across

the tester bed at her. "You know, it's okay to be sick. It's okay to let your guard down. It took me a long time to figure that out, but I'm telling you, there is no shame in needing other people."

Willa dropped her bag on the bed, then turned to her friend. "I know I need help, but I can't let my guard down with Lucas. I'm so afraid I'll hurt him."

Lorna pushed a hand through her braided hair. "I think you've already managed to do that. And to think, Lacey and I were worried that he'd be the one to hurt you."

"I'm sorry, Lorna. I tried to make him see that we couldn't have a relationship right now, that my future was too uncertain. But he wouldn't listen."

"Of course he wouldn't. Lucas has always followed his own path. He follows his heart. But this time, I think he's serious. I've never seen him like this."

Willa walked around the bed, took Lorna's hands in hers. "Can't you see why I'm doing this? Even if I come through the surgery with no signs of any other lumps, even if everything goes all right, there's still a chance that I won't be completely well. I'll have to go through months and months of treatment. I'll probably lose my hair, lose weight, get sick from the treatments. Lucas would want to be right there, and I can't bear putting him through that. I don't want him to start resenting me, to watch me wither away."

Lorna frowned. "So you're more concerned about how you'll look physically than having someone to help you through this?"

Shaking her head, Willa pulled away. "Of course

not. My goodness, I'm not that shallow, even though my job does require that kind of attitude. I don't want Lucas to see me that way, no, but it's more than just for the sake of my precious appearance, my image.'' Closing her eyes, she swallowed the lump in her throat. ''Lorna...''

''You're in love with my brother, aren't you?'' Lorna asked, awe in the question.

Willa couldn't speak. She nodded, tears pricking at her eyes. Finally she whispered the word. ''Yes.''

Lorna gently tugged her onto the bed, then sat next to her. ''And you don't want him to know?''

She shook her head. ''I don't want him to love me back.''

''Why?''

Willa opened her eyes, looked at her dear friend. ''I have to go and find my birth mother—I need to know why she gave me away, I need to know if she ever had breast cancer, and I guess I need to see her, just in case.''

''Just in case you don't survive this.''

''Yes. And...if I tell Lucas I love him, he'll follow me and he'll support me. I know that. I know him. But if things take a bad turn—''

''He'll be all alone again.''

Willa saw the complete understanding in her friend's eyes and breathed a sigh of relief. ''I've tried to explain to him. Lorna, he's suffered so much, just like you and Lacey. But Lucas has kept his fears and his hurt hidden so well—''

''He does put on a good front.''

''So can't you understand—it would devastate

him. I can't ask him to stay tied to a sick, possibly dying woman. It's not fair.''

"Is it ever?'' Lorna asked, compassion in her eyes. "Look at me, Willa. Look how long I fought against love, against any kind of intimacy. And then Mick came along and now—'' She stopped, held a hand to her stomach. "And now I'm going to have his child.''

Willa's tears turned to tears of joy. "Oh, Lorna. How wonderful! Does Mick know?''

Lorna nodded, her tears glistening brightly in the noonday light. "We haven't told anyone else yet, though. But I'm telling you, to prove to you that there is always hope. You need to change your attitude. Instead of expecting the worst, you need to concentrate on hoping for the best. Because believe me, if you open yourself up to the possibilities of all of God's blessings, the best is yet to come.''

The possibilities. That's what Lucas had wanted her to see, too. But right now, her only possibility was to survive this disease. And after that...

Willa hugged her friend. "I'm happy for you, and I understand what you mean. I've come so close to finding happiness here at Bayou le Jardin, and thanks to all of you, I have a strong sense of faith now. And I'll cherish each and every memory. But until I straighten out all the excess baggage in my life, I can't make a full commitment to Lucas.''

"Can't, or won't?''

Willa wiped her eyes, then got up. "I'm afraid, Lorna. I'll admit that. So afraid. And Lucas was right about one thing—it has much more to do with loving him than it does with fighting cancer.''

''I used to be the same,'' Lorna told her. ''So I certainly can't judge you. Take all the time you need, Willa. Go find your birth mother, have your surgery and then concentrate on getting well. But don't waste too much time—it's too precious. Like you said, each memory should be cherished. You have to make the most of whatever time God has granted you. And you have every right to find a little happiness, even if you only have a short while to enjoy it. So hurry. Lucas will be here, waiting.''

''Will he?''

''Knowing my brother, yes. He won't be waiting patiently, but he'll be waiting. I think he's been waiting for you all of his life. Please don't let him down.''

''That's exactly why I'm leaving,'' Willa said.

Lorna didn't try to stop her. Instead, she reached to the nightstand and picked up a Bible. ''You're going to miss church this morning. Take this with you.''

Willa took the leather-bound book, tears brimming in her eyes. ''Thank you for everything.''

Then she reached for her bag and headed out the door.

Chapter Fourteen

"How long is he going to stay out there in the swamp?"

Lorna looked across the glass counter at her sister. She rarely came to Lacey's shop, but today she'd felt restless, had needed to get out and walk. She was worried about Lucas. "It's been two days since Willa left, and not a word from either her—or Lucas, for that matter."

Lacey finished cataloging the new shipment of silk shawls she told Lorna she'd found at an estate sale in East Texas, then turned to her sister. "You know Lucas. He'll surface when he's good and ready and not a day sooner. But I have to admit, this time I'm worried about him, too. He's never reacted this way toward a woman."

"He's in love," Lorna said, tugging a teal-colored shawl off the walnut hall tree Lacey had tossed it across. Putting the shimmering shawl over her denim sundress, she eyed herself in the oval standing mirror. "This is nice."

"And it will go to a paying customer," Lacey said, a tart smile on her face. "So you haven't heard from Willa?"

"No. I only know what she told me before she left. That the mass was malignant and Dr. Savoie had advised a lumpectomy. That at least means she won't be disfigured and she probably won't have to deal with reconstructive surgery. She'll have a scar, but that's a small price to pay."

"If they can get all the cancerous cells," Lacey reminded her. "It must be terrible, waiting, wondering, not knowing. I mean, even going through treatment and having a doctor tell you the cancer is all gone—that doesn't mean it can't come back."

Lorna nodded, placed the delicate shawl on the hall tree's brass peg. "That's why she broke things off with Lucas—the uncertainty of it all. But he doesn't see it that way."

"That's because he wants to help her through this. He thinks if he's right there, fighting for her, he can save her. The same way he's always tried to fight for us."

Reaching for one of the decadent samples of chocolate Lacey sold in the shop, Lorna closed her eyes and nibbled the rich, dark confection. "Willa is afraid she'll just put him through agony. Her way of thinking is that if things don't go in a positive way, Lucas will be stuck with a very sick woman. I don't think she wants him to see her that way, to remember her like that."

Lacey adjusted some priceless eighteenth-century silver candelabras that graced a long mahogany sideboard, then added a pink- and green-tinged rare Hull vase to the mix. "Very noble of her, but kind of ridiculous, don't you think?"

"I tried to tell her. And I know, according to what little she told me, Lucas tried to make her see reason, but she's not thinking very clearly right now. She's only focused on all the negatives—her birth mother, the cancer, her distant parents."

"Speaking of her parents—shouldn't we call them?"

"She promised me she'd call them when she got to New York."

"Think she will?"

"I don't know. As Aunt Hilda would say, Willa is not using good sense right now. Her very life is in jeopardy, but she's so afraid of showing any signs of weakness, of asking for help, that she's running from everyone."

Lacey made a wry face. "Then she should fit right in with this bunch, don't you think?"

Lorna laughed, then touched a finger to the coveted teal shawl again. "Are you sure you won't cut me a deal on this shawl? I could really put it to good use when Mick gets home."

"Spare me the details," Lacey retorted. "And when is that lovable husband of yours coming back, anyway?"

"The end of the week," Lorna replied, wrapping her hands around her stomach. Her head down, she held her hands there for a minute, her mind on the baby she was carrying. "I can't wait to see him."

Lacey stopped rearranging knickknacks and went still. Lorna felt her sister's crystal-blue eyes centered on her face. "What's the matter with you?"

"You're glowing," Lacey said in a small, strained voice. "Lorna, are you pregnant?"

Lorna let out a gasp. "How did you know?"

Lacey came around the counter to get a closer look. "Because that's exactly the way I looked when I was carrying Neil's child. I used to stand in front of the mirror, my hands on my belly, just that way. And with that same expression on my face."

Wanting to kick herself for being such a dolt, Lorna hugged Lacey close. "I'm sorry. I wanted to tell you, really I did. But I wanted Mick to be the first to know, so I told him the other night right after Doc Howard confirmed it. But we've hardly had a chance to celebrate. With all this happening with Lucas and Willa, I just couldn't seem to find the right time to let y'all in on it. I did tell Willa before she left. I was hoping it would cheer her up, make her see that finding happiness is not that impossible, after all."

She stood back to study Lacey's pale face. "I wish you could have carried your baby to full term, Lacey."

"Lance." Lacey pulled away, hung against the counter. "His name was Lance—you know that." She stood there, her hands gripping the bright glass so tightly, her knuckles turned white. "It's all right to say his name. I wanted to keep up the tradition, you know, of having all these confusing L names. Neil and I laughed about it, how Aunt Hilda got all of us confused and how with a new baby named Lance, she'd be even more confused.''

"But she would have loved that. And so would Mamma and Daddy. They named us that way deliberately, remember.''

"Yes, I remember. Mamma said it was so lyrical, when she called all of us in to supper—Lacey, Lucas, Lorna.'' Then she whirled to face Lorna, a soft smile on her lips. "You could name your baby Lance.''

Lorna's heart went out to her sister. Lacey had so much love to give, and yet she'd built such an impeccable shell around her heart. "I couldn't do that. That was your baby. That's the name on his little grave.''

Wiping her eyes, Lacey managed a smile. "Well, then you'd better come up with some L names very soon. Oh, Lorna, I am so happy for you and Mick. And Mick—he must just be so thrilled. And very eager to get home to you.''

Glad that her sister was putting on a good show of support in spite of her miscarriage late in her pregnancy, Lorna fingered the shawl again. "Which is why I need something pretty to wear when he does get home. I was so nervous about telling him—isn't that silly? And now I'm nervous about seeing him again.''

"That's not silly,'' Lacey said, picking up the shawl to wrap it around Lorna's slender shoulders. "That's natural. Having a child is scary, amazing, wonderful. Take the shawl as a gift from me. Enjoy the time you have with your husband, this special time. Enjoy the baby growing in your tummy, too."

Lorna didn't have to hear what her sister was thinking. Because you never know when it might all end.

Lacey had once had it all, a loving husband, a baby on the way, and then her whole life had changed. Yet another tragedy for her strong-willed, beautiful older sister to deal with. Wanting so much for Lacey to again find someone to love, Lorna thought, at least for now, maybe they should help their wayward brother find some happiness.

"We have to get Lucas and Willa back together," she said. "Even if they have just a little while, even if she gets worse. Lucas wants that. He wants to be with her, no matter what."

"That's what a real commitment is all about," Lacey said. "I had that with Neil. And now you have that with Mick."

Lorna touched a hand to her sister's shoulder, her eyes settling on the antique diamond and filigree ring Neil had given Lacey for their engagement. "I hope you find someone again one day, Lacey."

Lacey shrugged, causing the delicate lace of her sundress to flutter around her shoulders. "Me? I've had my happy times and I have my memories."

"But you deserve more."

Pushing her out the door, Lacey said, "Well, don't dwell on me. Right now we have to find a way to get our brother back on solid ground. Lucas needs us. And he needs lots of prayer. More than he ever has. Let's see what we can do to remedy this situation between Willa and him.''

''That might be easier said than done,'' Lorna replied.

''We'll ask Aunt Hilda.''

''And she'll tell us to mind our own business.''

''And then she'll put on her prayer warrior hat and get on the job.''

Lorna grinned. ''Now there's a thought. If anyone can fix this, Aunt Hilda can.''

Lacey waved her out the door. ''With God's help.''

''Lord, I'm gonna need your help on this one,'' Lucas said into the early morning heat.

He was in his secret garden, sitting in the pagoda where he'd brought Willa. Had that only been a week or so ago? It seemed like he'd lived a whole lifetime in just a few short days. Lived, and lost yet again.

His sad little garden looked the same. The vegetation was lush and damp. Yellow wildflowers grew out of a nearly dead gnarled cypress knee. In the muddy marshes, orange calla lilies, greedy with moisture and bright with new flowers, sprouted and blossomed in the rich black loam near the water's edge. And across the way, a brown and white osprey sat in the low mist, its hawk eyes hooded and watchful as it waited for the perfect prey to come along just in time for breakfast.

Lucas gave a nod of respect to the noble bird. He should probably stay still and quiet, so the magnificent hawk could find some food. But Lucas needed to talk. Out loud.

The tiny bell chimes barely moved, but he heard the sound of their sighing song anyway. He knew they were there. Their melancholy chant suited his mood just fine.

"I found the woman of my dreams, then learned that she might be sick with a dreaded disease. And learned that the woman of my dreams is gun-shy about being the woman of my dreams."

Pointing a finger toward the sky, he asked, "What are You planning on doing about that one, Lord?"

A commotion behind Lucas caused the hawk to fly over the marsh. A cry of frustration expressed the bird's irritation.

Lucas felt that same irritation as he turned to find Roy Boy helping Aunt Hilda up the path. "What are you doing here?"

"I tried to tell her it was dangerous, dat she might fall, but she made me bring her here anyway."

Lucas shot the young man a look of complete sympathy. "She never listens to reason, for true."

Hilda stopped on the path, leaning heavily on her cane while she caught her breath. "And just who are you to make such pointed observations regarding my stubborn nature?"

Lucas grinned, shrugged. "*Moi,* I'm just a lonely, lost man who came out here to find some peace and quiet."

Hilda nodded. "Roy Boy, you can leave us now."

Roy Boy rolled his eyes. "My mamma told me da stay right with you."

Hilda held a hand on one hip, regarding the boy with a hard glare. "And I'm telling you to go. Lucas will see me home." She waited for her nephew to confirm this.

Which he didn't. "I wasn't planning on coming up to the mansion today, Auntie."

Hilda waved a hand. "As I just said, Lucas will see me home." She turned to gaze at Lucas, her chin jutting in defiance.

He lifted a brow, then let out a heavy sigh. "I will see her home, Roy Boy. Go tell your mamma that."

The kid gave them a look, then turned down the winding path, shaking his head all the way.

"How did you know I'd be here?" Lucas asked, his gaze moving across the water. He wondered where the osprey had gone.

"I'm old and I'm aching," Aunt Hilda said as she made her way into the pagoda, taking the hand Lucas offered her. "But I'm not blind. And I know my children like I know this bayou. I just figured you'd come to the one place where you felt close to God."

"Is that why you showed me this place all those years ago? So I could find God?"

"Maybe." She sat beside him, letting out a breath, her cane balanced in front of her. "Or maybe I just thought you needed some place to call your own."

He lifted his hands high in the air, then let them drop to his sides. "This is my place, all right. Lost, sad, overgrown. Kinda like me, I reckon."

"You're none of those things." She didn't speak for a while, just sat there, her hands on her cane, facing straight ahead. Then she turned to him.

"When were you planning on coming home, anyway?"

Lucas finally looked at her, then rubbed the beard stubble on his face. He hadn't slept much or eaten much. He hadn't cared much. "I am home," he told her with a sweeping gesture. "I think this is where I belong. Lost deep in the bayou."

"This is a good place to hide from your troubles, I suppose."

"No, it's a good place to get away from people," he replied. "A man needs some downtime, you know what I mean?"

"I know exactly what you mean. But you can't fool me, Lucas. You're pouting."

He got up, spun around in a little dance that caused the bell chimes to shake and shimmy, his hands clapping against his knees. "Yes, I am doing that, exactly that. You see, I fell in love with this beautiful lady, laid my soul open at her feet, offered to dedicate my life to her, and she just walked away. She doesn't want the likes of Lucas Dorsette in her life."

Hilda glanced at him, waited for him to stop dancing, then stared long and hard. "Did you really listen to a word that woman said to you?"

He nodded. "*Oui,* I listened. And I heard loud and clear. So if you don't mind, I'd like to go back to pouting now."

Hilda shook her head, then lifted her cane to poke him on the leg.

"Ouch!"

"I should hit you on that hard head of yours. Sit down and listen to me, Lucas."

He did as he was told. He knew if he didn't listen, she'd sit right there until he did. "What?"

"Willa is going through one of the worst things a young woman can," Aunt Hilda began. "She has breast cancer. Now, I know you think you understand what that means, but think again. Here's a woman who's relied on her looks for most of her life, for her living. Here's a beautiful young person who's just found out she has a devastating, life-threatening disease. She's frightened, she's scared and she needs to get well. But what do you do—oh, you offer her comfort and support, but with stipulations. You want more. You're in love with her, so you want her to make a commitment to that love."

"Is that too much to ask?" Lucas shouted, amazement etched in his haggard features. "I want her to survive. I want to be there with her, to make sure she fights. I don't want her to give up, not now, not when I've only just—"

"Only just begun to love her?" Aunt Hilda finished for him.

"Yes, yes." He bobbed his head, then scissored his fingers through his tousled hair. "I love her, Aunt Hilda. I love her, but I might not have a chance to prove that love to her. I might lose her before we've even had a fair chance. I don't want to lose her." He stilled, then looked over the cypress trees and moss-draped vines. "I tried to tell her how I felt."

Hilda reached a hand to him. "And that's the very reason she walked out of your life. You were smothering her, Lucas. You—you can be overwhelming on a good day. But coupled with everything she's dealing with, you were like a tidal wave, pushing her out of control.''

He shot his aunt a sideways glance. ''You mean I came on too strong?''

''That's what I believe. You scared her away.''

''But I only wanted her to know how I felt.''

''She knows, but she's afraid. Can you imagine what must be going through her mind right now? How will she come out of this—all in one piece, or cut up, her body mutilated? How will she get through the treatments, the sickness, the nausea, the hair loss? And what if, after all that, she still doesn't go into remission? What then, Lucas? Willa is very proud. She doesn't want you to see her like that, she doesn't want to put you through that.''

''I wouldn't care,'' he told her. ''I'd only see the woman I love.''

''Are you sure about that?''

Lucas looked at his aunt's loving eyes, then he sank onto the bench beside her. ''I'd hope I'd be able to deal with whatever came along.'' He was silent as he thought over the last few days. He'd never really looked past keeping Willa safe and intact. ''Of course, in my mind, I was willing everything to be all right. I willed her not to really have cancer. And I didn't think beyond that. I only thought about how I feel whenever I'm with her. I only knew that I would protect her and keep her safe if she'd let me.''

Hilda patted his arm. ''You can't will something to be so, Lucas. Only God can determine that.''

''Well, I can sure fight against God's will, then, can't I?''

"Yes, but you won't win. You never have before."

He should have known Aunt Hilda knew him better than he knew himself. She'd probably figured him out a long time ago. "Tell me about it. Seems I've failed miserably at fighting with God."

"You haven't failed at anything, except maybe learning how to understand God. All this time you've been fighting against him, blaming him for what happened to your parents, He's been listening and He's been right here with you. You've had a good life, Lucas. You have never once done anything to make me think you're a failure."

He couldn't look at her. The love he felt for his aunt at that moment was so overwhelming, so powerful, he only wanted to let it soak over him like a cleansing rain. "I could have done more. I should have—"

"Don't be bitter, Lucas. Don't hide away, wondering what might have been."

"Then what do you suggest I do?"

Aunt Hilda got up, leaned on her cane. "I think we should call Willa's parents, tell them we care about Willa, make sure they know what's going on. Then I think we should back off."

He stood, stumbled against the door frame. "So we just do nothing? We don't even try to help Willa?"

"We can help her more by keeping her in our prayers while we honor her wishes," Aunt Hilda replied. "She won't like that we meddled and called her parents, but they need to be told. She will need them there."

"But not us, at least not me?" It was the same, always the same. He lived on the fringes. He wasn't part of the details. His sisters always managed to shut him out. Now his aunt, whom he loved and respected with all his heart, was suggesting the same thing.

"*You* are much more than Willa can deal with right now. You're just going to have to be patient."

Lucas helped his aunt out of the small enclosure. As they walked slowly down the path, he said, "She won't come back to me. She's using all of these other problems as a smokescreen. She doesn't want to feel the same way about me as I feel about her. But I'm not ready to accept that."

"Your heart is hurting right now," Hilda said. "But soon, everything will work out."

"One way or another, right?"

"Yes," she replied. "We have to accept whatever happens, good or bad." She tugged him by the hand. "Come home, Lucas. Your sisters are worried about you."

He went home, but he wasn't going to be patient. Nor was he going to sit around and do nothing. He was tired of living on the edge. He wanted to show his family that he could be a responsible human being. After a long hot shower and a shave, he headed to the restaurant to find Lorna.

"Have you heard from Willa?" he asked, while his sister moved around the kitchen, instructing her staff on preparations for the early lunch crowd.

Lorna barely glanced up. "I'm busy, Lucas. Glad you're back among the living, but very busy."

"Non, belle." He grabbed the sleeve of her white chef jacket. "Don't give me the brush-off. I'll only badger you until you tell me."

Lorna nodded at Emily. "The turtle soup looks good." Then she turned to face her brother. "Okay. She called last night. She's okay. Just making preparations, of course."

"That's a relief."

"And Lucas—" she touched a hand to his arm "—from everything she told me, there's a very good chance that she'll come through this and survive. They found the lump in time, thanks to her self-examination and the mammogram. That's something to be thankful for."

"Yes, yes, it is." Then he had to ask. "Where is she, Lorna? Is she at her apartment or at her parents' estate?"

Lorna glanced around the kitchen, hesitated. "I don't think I should tell you that."

Lucas bent his head low so his next words would be for his sister's ears only. "Did she find her birth mother? Did they talk?"

"I don't know," Lorna admitted. "She…she was very short with me. Just the facts about the surgery. She didn't mention the rest."

"And her parents?"

"Aunt Hilda called them this morning. Told them everything and also told them she took full responsibility for being the bearer of bad news. But fortunately, Willa had already contacted them. They're on their way home now."

Lucas closed his eyes in relief. "I'm glad Willa got up the courage to call them. That's a good sign, at least."

"Yes, it is."

"Is she at their estate, then?"

"Lucas, you promised you'd back off, remember?"

"Yeah, I know. But I need to see her, Lorna. I need to see her one last time before she has the surgery. Then I'm going to leave her alone."

"I don't know—"

"Just tell me where she is?"

Lorna gave him a concerned look. "I want you two to work things out, but Aunt Hilda seems to think we need to let Willa get through this first. And now that her parents are coming home—"

"I have to see her again. Just...to tell her one thing."

"Oh, and what's that?"

Lucas moved out of the way as a waiter came by with the dessert tray. "I need to tell her that I understand now. And that I'm willing to wait for her. I'm impatient and I'm hurting, but I don't want her to go into surgery thinking I'm bitter and angry. I wasn't so nice when she left, but I'm better now. I want Willa to know that whenever she's ready, I'll be here, right here. And if she's never ready, well, I'll just have to deal with that, too." Somehow.

"That could help her during recovery," Lorna reasoned. "They say attitude is important with cancer patients."

Glad he was making sense at last, Lucas plowed on. "Yes, that's what I mean. If Willa goes into this still upset by what happened between us, she might not recover as quickly. And then I'd blame myself. She's already very negative about things—thinking the worst. I need to tell her—there's just so much I need to say to her."

"And then you'll leave her alone, give her time to heal?"

"Yes."

It would be hard, but he'd have to do it. He didn't have any choice. What Aunt Hilda had said made sense. He had been smothering Willa, and she wasn't used to that kind of intimate attention. She didn't buy into it because the only kind of attention she'd ever had was the distant kind. The kind that sold magazines and carried fashion shows. The kind that her well-meaning but cold parents had barely given her. He had to let her go in order to win her back. It was his only chance. That and the hope that she really did care about him.

Lorna nodded. "She's at her parents' estate. That's all I know right now."

"That's enough," Lucas replied, heading out the door. "That's enough, sister love." He gave her a quick salute, then called, "I'm going to New York."

Lacey came into the restaurant, glancing over her shoulder at her retreating brother. "Where's he headed in such an all-fire hurry?"

"To a place where they've never seen the likes of

him," Lorna told her. "He's going to New York to see Willa."

Lacey's blue eyes widened. "He is?" She smiled, then turned to her sister. "Aunt Hilda isn't going to like this. Did you urge him to go?"

"No, I advised against it, but he wouldn't listen. Think I did the right thing, telling him where Willa is?"

Lacey put a hand on her sister's shoulder. "I think that no matter what advice we give him, he's going to do what he wants anyway."

Lorna looked into the sun-dappled garden. "Well, right now, he only wants to see Willa one more time before she goes into surgery."

"I hope he makes it in time," Lacey said. "Does he know she's scheduled to go in for the surgery in New York in two days?"

"No," Lorna admitted. "I didn't tell him that part."

Chapter Fifteen

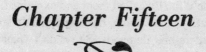

It was well past midnight. Willa stood at the terrace doors, staring onto the moonlit gardens of the home where she'd spent part of her teen and adult years. It was a lovely house, a Georgian style manor, with cultured yards, tennis courts, stables and a shimmering swimming pool. But then, there had been many such houses. She remembered them. Her family had moved up the social ladder about as quickly as the grass grew in the sloping, cultivated yard.

Had she ever really had a home to call her own?

She thought about Bayou le Jardin and how safe and secure she'd felt there. Thought about Lucas's secret garden and his primitive cabin on the bayou. Had she only been there for a few days? And how could a few short days change a person so completely?

And now, it seemed as if she'd lived yet another lifetime since coming back to New York.

She was tired, so very tired.

"You should be in bed, dear."

Willa whirled to find her mother standing in the open doorway, dressed for bed in exquisite black silk and lace.

"I couldn't sleep," Willa said, turning to the window.

As she'd expected, her parents had been concerned when she'd finally called them and explained. They'd immediately come home, had immediately started issuing orders and demands. She didn't want to hear anything else tonight, though. Tonight, right now, she wanted to stand here and think about Lucas. They'd almost had a chance, but now…

For an instant, Willa thought she heard the roar of an airplane in the distance. *His* airplane. Just imagining things, she supposed.

Her mother's soft voice interrupted her thoughts. "Are you worried about the surgery? Willa, we can bring in someone else—"

"Dr. Carlton is doing the surgery, Mother. We've already been over this. He's one of the best."

"Well, yes, but if we'd known about this sooner—"

"You would have clouded the issue, made things much worse," Willa told her. Then, because she didn't want to seem harsh, she added, "I know you mean well, but everything is in place. I've consulted oncologists, pathologists and two very capable cancer surgeons, and they all agree that I have a good chance of surviving this."

She needed to tell her adoptive mother the rest of the story. Right now, Willa was too shocked and saddened to tell her mother what she'd found out about her birth mother. Yet her parents had a right to know.

Candace O'Connor advanced into the room in a whirl of expensive perfume and a rush of rustling heavy silk. "But there has to be more we can do. There has to be something. I still can't understand why you went all the way down to Louisiana to get a second opinion when you know perfectly well that your father is friends with some of the best doctors in the country."

"Yes, I know that, Mother." *Because you make it a point to drop their names at cocktail parties and holiday balls. How could I forget?*

"Dear, you're going to have to tell me again, just who are these people you've befriended down there?"

"The Dorsettes," Willa said, her arms folded against her body defensively. "They were very kind to me."

"Strangers, though, darling. They are complete strangers."

"Not to me," Willa said. "They were…are…my friends."

"Well, regardless of all of that, your father and I are here now, and we're going to see you through this. I just wish there was something else I could do or say."

Hearing the genuine worry in her mother's voice, Willa turned. "I've done everything possible, Mother." She hesitated, then added, "Including trying to find my birth mother."

Candace brought a hand to the pearls at her throat. "Oh, my."

"Oh, my, indeed," Willa said. She was about to tell her mother exactly what she'd found when the sound she'd heard outside became very apparent. It was the roar of an engine. Willa looked out the window, saw the shimmering lights of a low-flying plane.

"What a commotion," Candace said, rushing to the window. "Willa, is that an airplane landing on our back lawn?"

Willa's heart hammered against her chest. She didn't want to believe it, but... "Yes, Mother, I think it is."

Together, they watched the bright yellow plane perform a sleek landing, coming in on the long, straight rear driveway and stopping in a quick skid in front of the tree line.

"That was cutting things close," Candace said, indignation coloring the words. "I think I'd better get your father."

Willa couldn't speak. She didn't believe her eyes.

Before Candace could find her sleeping husband, the doorbell rang, its chimes echoing throughout the still house.

"Who on earth?" Candace hurried to the open doors leading from the living room. She didn't answer the front door across the marble-tiled hallway, though. To Willa's amazement, her mother looked startled.

Willa waited, heard voices, then saw the sleepy

butler heading with a solemn, disapproving expression on his face toward her mother.

"Mister—"

"Lucas Dorsette," Lucas said as he moved in front of the butler and took Candace's hand in his. "You must be Mrs. O'Connor. I've come to see your daughter."

"Lucas?" Willa didn't realize she'd spoken until Lucas looked across the room at her.

Then he pushed past her mother. "Willa."

He came toward her, wearing jeans and a lightweight black jacket. He looked tired, haggard, ragged.

And wonderful.

"You're here," she said, knowing she sounded redundant. She was glad he was here, so glad. But she also knew he shouldn't have come. "What are you doing? Why did you come?"

"I needed to see you," he said. Then he glanced over his shoulder at her hovering mother. "Alone."

Candace waved a hand. "Young man—did you just land a plane in my yard?"

"Lucas. My name is Lucas," he said to her mother, his eyes never leaving Willa's face. "Yes, I landed a plane in your yard, because I'm in love with your daughter, Mrs. O'Connor. And I just wanted her to know that before she goes into surgery. And I need to tell her a few other things, too, if you don't mind."

Completely at a loss for words, Candace ran a hand over her silvery blond bob. "Well, I—"

"I knew you'd understand," Lucas said, turning to give her a dazzling smile. "I'm not going to hang around too long. I'm a long way from home and I'm tired—it was a really hard flight—but I've got to do this. If you could give me five minutes, just five minutes, I'd be so grateful.''

Willa watched him. The whole time he talked, he gently guided her mother toward the hallway. Then, before her flabbergasted mother could breathe a word of protest, he pushed her into the hall and, still smiling, closed the double doors into the living room. Then he turned to Willa. ''She seems nice enough.''

''I can't believe you're really here,'' Willa said, his words—''I'm in love with your daughter''—playing over and over in her mind. She pointed toward the plane. ''How—''

''The Piper, of course. Flew it right up the countryside in two days' time. Had to land and refuel about every three hundred or so miles and catch some sleep to keep the FAA cool, but it purred like a kitten all the way. I made my sister tell me where you were.''

He'd flown the Piper all the way up here to see her. Willa could only shake her head. ''Why?''

He came to the window, took her hands in his. ''You look so pretty.''

Willa glanced at her heavy blue satin wrapper and matching gown. ''Must be the lighting. My mother knows all the tricks.''

''No trick of the light, love.'' He tugged her into his arms. ''You are and will always be so beautiful to me.''

Her heart fluttered. She closed her eyes and savored being in his arms. ''Sounds like a song.''

"Being with you is like a song."

Willing herself to snap out of it, Willa pulled away from him. "Why are you here, Lucas?"

"Not for the reasons you think," he said, backing away. "I didn't come to conquer, Willa. I came to let you go."

She hadn't expected that, especially since he'd told her mother he was in love with Willa. "What do you mean?"

He raked a hand through his curling dark locks. "Aunt Hilda set me straight about a few things. Said I needed to give you some breathing room. So… that's what I'm doing."

Willa didn't know whether to laugh or cry. "So you came all this way just to tell me that?"

He nodded. "Yes. That's it. You're free. I won't push you anymore. I really don't have the right, do I?"

She saw the hurt in his dark eyes. "You're so wrong, Lucas. I'm the one who doesn't have any rights here. I'm the one who has to let you go."

"That was my line," he said. "But I understand…about everything. You have a lot of heavy things to deal with. I don't want to be a part of that mix. But I…I did want you to know that I love you. And that's that."

Willa felt as if she had been released into thin air. Without a net. Was he letting her down gently? Had he come all this way to tell her this because he'd finally realized what she'd known all along—that they didn't have a future together? Even if they did love each other?

"I'm glad you're beginning to see things my way," she told him, though her words didn't hold a strong conviction. "It's good that we can get it over with now. Before things get worse."

"I guess so. Especially since one of us isn't willing to give it a chance."

"And that one would be me?"

"It sure ain't me, baby."

Telling herself she should be glad he was being so reasonable, Willa looked over the night. "I'm having the surgery in the morning."

She heard his sharp intake of breath but she didn't dare turn around. She didn't dare beg him to stay here with her, either. So she set her shoulders and told him in a calm voice, "I'm glad you came, Lucas. But it was really unnecessary."

He huffed a breath. "Unnecessary? Is that how you really feel about me? That it's all been just a big waste of time?"

Deciding she should finish this once and for all, Willa pivoted to glare at him. "Yes. A big waste of time. You see, in spite of the doctors' high hopes, my future doesn't look so bright."

He touched her then, a hand on her arm. And she saw in his eyes, felt in that touch, just how hard he was fighting. "Why is that, love?"

She stood, her hands at her sides, feeling the warmth of his fingers on her arm. "Because I went to visit my birth mother. But I was too late."

His other arm came up and he pulled her close. "What happened?"

She looked at him, tried to smile. "She died about

ten years ago. From breast cancer. She was thirty-two years old.''

''Willa.'' For a minute, he stood looking at her as if he knew exactly where this left things between them. Then he tugged her into his arms, one hand pulling through her hair. ''Willa?''

''I talked to her sister—my aunt. My mother—her name was Elsie—had me when she was only sixteen. Her boyfriend abandoned her for another woman, refused to acknowledge the pregnancy. That's why she gave me up. Her family decided it was for the best. She never got married, never had another child. But in the end—when the cancer came—her family stuck by her just as they'd done when she gave me up. They didn't abandon her, at least. I can take some comfort in that, I suppose.''

''Willa, I'm so sorry.''

There was no more pretense, no more noble declarations between them. He held her, rocking her, soothing her, his hands moving through her hair. For a long time, he didn't speak. He just held her.

Willa knew she would always remember this moment, this time of being in his arms. It would be the last time he'd ever hold her this way. Everything would change come morning. Everything. But right now, it felt so good to be in his arms.

Because it did feel so right, she forced herself away. ''You should go.''

''I don't think I can do that—not now.''

''You have to go, Lucas. Just go.''

''I won't leave you like this. I thought I could, but I can't.''

He reached for her, but she moved away. Clutching the back of a leather chair, she looked at him. "My odds just got worse. So I want you to leave now, Lucas. You said you would. You said you came here to reassure me, not to pressure me."

He dropped his hands to his sides. "I came here because I love you and I want to be with you, for better or worse. I was making one last effort to win your heart."

She couldn't speak. She just shook her head. She couldn't tell him he'd had her heart all along.

"At least let me stay until you're out of surgery tomorrow."

She held tightly to the chair, her head down. "No. You said you came here to let me go, to give me some space and some peace. Don't change your mind now. Don't do this to me or yourself, Lucas."

He stood there, an arm's length away, his expression filled with the dilemma he faced. "You're right. I came here to give you hope. I want you to fight. I want you to know that I love you, no matter what. So you'll get well and come back to me, whenever you're ready."

She turned to the window. "I thought we might have a chance, but not now." She whirled to face him, her heart in each word she spoke. "It could get bad, Lucas. I don't want you here when it does."

He started for her, then bent his head, shrugged. Finally, he said, "You really don't know me at all, do you, Willa?"

Then he turned and left the room.

She heard the front door shut and she fell into the

chair she'd been holding with a white-knuckled grip. She wanted to cry but she was too numb. Sending him away had been the hardest thing she'd ever done. But what choice did she have?

She didn't move until she heard the plane cranking up, until she knew he'd turned it and lifted it over the trees.

"Lucas," she whispered as she watched the Piper's lights grow dim, "I do know you. And I love you, too."

"You're beginning to show." Lucas clutched his baby sister close, kissed her red-blond hair. "How you feeling?"

"Better than you look," Lorna told him as they walked outside together. It was a beautiful Sunday morning in September. "Are you coming to church with us?"

"*Non.* I'm going to head out." He motioned with his hands, indicating he didn't know which way he was going. He hadn't been clear on that since the night he'd left Willa in New York, well over six weeks ago.

"Aunt Hilda won't be happy."

"Well, it won't be the first time I've disappointed her, now, will it?"

"I'm sorry, Lucas."

"For what?"

"That things didn't work out between Willa and you. I sure thought…"

"*Oui,* me, too, *chère.* I thought a lot of things. But, hey, tomorrow comes another day, *hein?*" He wanted to ask her if she'd heard from Willa, but then, he didn't want to know if she had. It would be too much to handle.

Lorna kissed his cheek, then walked over to where Mick waited for her by his truck. Lucas watched as her husband kissed her, then touched his hand to her stomach.

"They look so happy, don't they?"

This time, it was Lacey talking. Lucas shrugged, held a hand to his eyes to shield them from the sun and maybe from the beautiful sight of his sister and her husband sharing an intimate moment together. "I reckon so."

"We're a pair," Lacey said, placing a slender arm around his shoulder. "You coming to church?"

"No, I am not. I just told Lorna that, so spare me the lecture."

"Excuse me," Lacey said. "And just for the record, I wasn't going to lecture you."

"Well, don't pity me, either. I'm doing just fine. Dandy, really."

"I can tell," she said, her hands swiping across his beard stubble. "You forgot to bring your razor again?"

"Yep." He pushed her away, then leaned close to kiss her cheek. "Get out of here."

"If you're not coming to church, you'd better get lost before Aunt Hilda comes out that door," Lacey warned.

His sister didn't have to tell him twice. Lucas took off walking, and in a matter of minutes, hot and bothered, he entered the cool serenity of his garden. The pagoda looked as weathered and sad as ever. And suited his mood just fine.

He'd been coming here a lot lately. Sometimes to remember. Sometimes to forget, as the song went. And yet he couldn't forget. He couldn't forget the woman he loved had pushed him away. Because she was sick. Because she was afraid. Because she didn't trust him to love her for better or worse, through sickness and health, till death do them part.

But he'd stayed right there by her side, in spite of her efforts to send him away. Willa might not ever know it, but he'd been there in the waiting room at the hospital, right along with her very formal, very polite, very worried parents—the same parents he'd badgered with early morning phone calls until they'd told him the name of the hospital. He had not left New York until he knew she was going to be all right.

All he knew was that she'd made it through the surgery and the doctors gave her strong odds of beating the cancer. So what was holding her back from coming to him?

"I couldn't will it so, Lord," he said, his voice echoing over the lush bayou. "I couldn't make things better. So...You know something? I'm tired. And I'm just gonna turn it over to You and...then maybe I can sleep at night. Maybe I can forget having her there with me in the cabin. Maybe if I tell You all my troubles, I'll get the scent of her perfume out of my pillow and the feel of her sweet lips out of my mind."

Silently, Lucas asked God to help him. Asked God

to make him see he'd never have Willa back. He didn't dare God, or defy Him, as he'd done so often in the past.

Instead, Lucas sat with his eyes shut and listened. Time seemed to stop, but the old sundial indicated it was almost time for church. He went still, perfectly still. And he remembered. All the pain of his childhood, all the lost hopes and empty paths, all the wild wishes and carefree prayers.

This prayer was earnest. This prayer was real.

"Just keep her safe, Lord. And keep her well. That's all I ask."

A hot morning breeze rustled the willow trees, pushed at the great cypress trees, teased the Spanish moss. The tiny bell chimes tinkled and sang their melancholy song. The osprey was back, sitting ever watchful on a stump across the way, but Lucas didn't stop to admire the lone hawk this morning. Soon it would be autumn, Indian summer. Then some respite from the intense heat.

And maybe some respite from all his memories.

He kept his eyes closed for a long time, trying not to think at all while he listened to the soft, melodious crying of the chimes.

He thought he smelled her scent.

Then he opened his eyes and saw her standing there, right at the edge of the secluded garden. "Willa?"

She walked toward him, wearing a straw hat and a floral sundress. And in spite of her pale skin and fragile appearance, she was smiling.

Lucas blinked. "Must be sunspots." But when he

opened his eyes, she was still there. Only she was closer.

"What are you doing here?" he asked, his voice cracked and hollow, dried up like the heat-soaked bayou.

"I came to find you," she said. Then she just stood there, watching him, her hands at her side, tears in her eyes. "I've missed you, Lucas."

He had to laugh at that. "Oh, yeah? Well, I missed you, too, *chère*." An understatement, but the truth. He'd burned with missing her. And he wasn't about to let his heart even hope. "Want to tell me what this is about, Willa?"

She came inside the tiny wooden structure, sank down beside him, then took his hand in hers. "You remember that night in your cabin?"

"Every waking minute," he said, refusing to enjoy the way her fingers laced with his.

"I made a promise that night, Lucas. I didn't tell you, but I promised myself and God that somehow I'd come back to you—both you and God."

He jerked his hand away. "It would have been nice if you'd shared that with me. Sure would have saved me some heartache."

"I couldn't tell you then," she said, her voice small and low. "And after I found out about my birth mother, I was even more afraid—"

He whirled then, went down on his knees in front of her, his fists at his chest. "You were afraid of dying? You were afraid of me? You were afraid of living, maybe? And you thought, gee, if I die, that will just make it so much easier, right?" When she didn't answer, he reached up to hold her by her arms. "Well, it hasn't been easy, Willa. I have worried and wondered and prayed. I tried to put my will ahead of God's will—to save you, to have you." He stopped, his eyes locking with hers. "I gave up."

She started to cry. "Don't give up. Please, Lucas, let me explain."

He could take anything but her tears. So he moved away, steeled his heart against them. "I should tell you what you told me in New York. I should tell you to go away."

"I'm not leaving, not this time," she said, wiping tears off her face. "I need to tell you…that I love you."

He didn't dare look at her. He rocked back, crouching on the floor. "And? Or should I say but? There's always a but."

"But…I was wrong to push you away. You will never know, never realize how hard that was for me."

"I think I have some inkling," he replied, anger and joy warring in his heart.

"I really meant what I said. I didn't want you to have to be the one to see me through this. But then—"

"What made you change your mind?"

"The song," she said. "And you." She was crying harder. "I came out of surgery and everything looked okay. The lumpectomy went well and…I just had to get through the first couple of treatments." She sighed, a soft, shuddering sound. "Then my mother told me about how you'd sat there in the waiting room with them. How you'd stayed silent and still. But you stayed. You stayed until you knew I was safe. Then you nodded to them and walked away.''

Lucas had to close his eyes again. ''I didn't want to go. I didn't want to leave you. But…I'd promised to let you go.''

He felt her fingers on his chin. ''The treatment has been rough, Lucas. I've had radiation and chemo, too. Because of my birth mother dying from breast cancer, the risk of my cancer coming back is strong, so they're giving me a double whammy just to be sure. But, do you know what's helped me during these treatments, during these last few weeks?''

He kept his eyes down, studying the bright blue and green floral cotton of her gathered dress. If he looked at her face, he might not have the strength to walk away again. But he had to ask. ''What helped you, Willa?''

He heard her swallow more tears. ''Knowing that you stayed there, even when I wanted you to leave— that kept me going through the treatments, the sick days, the reality of this disease. I remembered what you said, right here in this garden. 'The beauty remains; the pain passes.' And that's why I had to come back.''

He looked up, realized why she was wearing a hat. Tears burned his eyes. He touched a hand to her face, her hat, his gaze moving over her features. ''Are you all right?''

''I'm doing okay,'' she said, sniffing back tears. ''I had to cut my hair—or what was left of my hair—

but I gave it to a company that makes wigs for children…with cancer.''

He held his hand on the hat, gritted his teeth. ''All that beautiful hair. Willa—''

''It gets to me sometimes, but so far, so good,'' she said, silencing him with two fingers on his lips. ''It'll grow back, Lucas. And luckily, I love hats.'' She dropped her hand, then wrapped it over his. ''But…that's not why I'm here. I never made it to church that Sunday, remember?''

He nodded. ''Aunt Hilda wasn't too pleased.''

She laughed, cried. ''I never got to hear the words to the song—the one you played that night.''

''So you came back for that?''

''I came back for you.''

He touched his other hand to her face, hope beginning to surface through all the murkiness. ''For better or worse?''

She bobbed her head. ''Dr. Carlton told me I had the wrong attitude. He said instead of feeling sorry for myself, I should take my status and…help other women who might be going through the same thing.'' She placed her hands on his head, touched her fingers through his hair. ''Then I had a long talk with my parents. I told them about my birth mother, how she'd died from this disease. How I was so afraid I wouldn't survive. Then I told them that I loved you but was afraid of telling you that.''

Lucas was listening. He could see the sincerity in her eyes. And in spite of her pallor, in spite of the hat covering her hair loss, he could also see the hope she held.

"What happened then?"

"My mother was amazing. I was so upset about losing you, I think she was worried it would affect my recovery. So she encouraged me to talk about you. I told her about the song and she went out and found a hymnal and she read me the words to 'Something Beautiful.' And then it all made sense. That night in the garden with Aunt Hilda, I was *full* of broken dreams and so much strife, but God was reaching out to me. I was still so scared, though.

"I told my mother everything—all about you and your wonderful family. I told her how much I loved you. We had such a good talk. She told me how much they both loved me. My father was crying—I've never seen him like that. He told me about the day they brought me home, how happy they were. They love me, Lucas. In their own way, they love me."

"Is that so hard to comprehend?"

"It was. For so long, it was. But now, now I know what I have to do."

He held his breath. She'd said she'd come back for him. She'd told him she loved him. Was she only coming back to leave again?

Before he could voice a question, she leaned down to place her forehead against the top of his head. "I'm going to survive, Lucas. And I'm going to help other women. I have some clout. I have friends and connections everywhere, and so do my parents. We're going to start a foundation for breast cancer research. And we're going to help other women who might not have as much clout or money as we do.

I'm going to be the spokesperson. I'm not going to feel sorry for myself anymore.''

Lucas looked at her. Sitting there with her big, floppy hat and her bright blue eyes, she'd never looked more beautiful. ''You thought of all the possibilities, didn't you?''

''Yes, I did. And I thought of you and how I'd hurt you. I'm so sorry, Lucas.'' She pulled his hands down, held them in her lap. ''If you're still willing to have me, I want to be with you. And...I don't care if we only have a few weeks, a few years, even a few days. I love you. That's all I need to know.''

Lucas fell on his knees, glanced skyward, then tugged her down with him. He kissed her, wiped her tears away, wiped his tears away. ''What took you so long?''

''I don't know,'' she said, kissing his face. ''I was just afraid.''

''You don't have to be afraid anymore. You're home now, love.''

Willa kissed him again, hugged him tight, then laughed. ''We've got to hurry. I saw Aunt Hilda at the house. She's expecting us in church. And she promised me I'd hear my song this time.''

''I'll sing it myself, if I have to. Or at least play it on my horn for you.'' Lucas helped her up, then held her in his arms. ''I can't believe this is real.''

''Lucas, we've got so many reasons to thank God.''

''I'm thanking Him right now,'' he told her as he nuzzled her neck. ''And I'll be thanking Him for a long time to come.''

They started down the path. "We have our whole lives together," Willa said, smiling. "I'm going to fight to make that happen." She stopped, looked at him. "You see, I finally realized I can't live without you."

Lucas nodded, took her in his arms to spin her around. "Now, love, that is something beautiful. *Je t'aime.*"

Off across the bayou, the osprey lifted its wings and flew toward the morning sun. Down below, two gray doves cooed at each other as they fluttered and hopped in the foliage. And in the pagoda, the bell chimes played a new melody.

Epilogue

One month later

"**M**y bride is so beautiful."

Lucas made the statement to anyone who happened to be within listening distance. He was surrounded by his family and his friends at his late-afternoon wedding, with fall leaves and the crisp scent and feel of autumn all around him. And his bride...well, beautiful was an understatement.

Willa was wearing a tea-length lightweight wool suit in a vanilla-rich shade of cream with a close-fitting hat that sported an enormous garnet filigree brooch and gave her the look of a 1920s socialite. She was a bit pale and willowy, but thankfully, she was doing great.

"She looks happy, doesn't she?" Lucas asked Lacey.

"Yes, and you look content," Lacey told him as

she kissed his cheek. "And quite handsome in that dapper tailored suit."

"I'm a very handsome man," Lucas joked, winking at her. "You made a lovely bridesmaid. You and Lorna both, of course."

Lacey looked at the russet-colored shantung suit she was wearing. "Well, Lorna might have been the matron of honor, but my tummy is flatter."

Seeing the longing in his big sister's eyes, Lucas pulled her close. "I want all of this for you, Lacey."

Lacey smiled, sighed, looked across the gardens where Lorna, Mick and Aunt Hilda were laughing and talking to Willa and her parents. "I had all of this, remember. I don't know if the Lord will allow such bliss twice in a lifetime."

"Wouldn't hurt to test the waters, find out," Lucas replied. "You're just too pretty and too loving to spend the rest of your life here on earth alone."

Lacey patted the chignon at the nape of her neck, then fingered the garnet-jeweled necklace Willa had given both her wedding attendants. "I'm not alone. I have you and Lorna, and Aunt Hilda, and the Babineaux family. And now I have Mick and Willa, too. And soon, a new niece or nephew to spoil."

Lucas wrapped an arm around her, tugging her with him toward his new bride. He couldn't stand to be more than a few feet away from Willa, but he knew his sister was hurting inside. "Someone should be spoiling you," he said in a low voice. "And I do believe that somewhere out there, there's a man waiting for you. A special man. A man only Lacey Dorsette can claim for her own."

Lacey laughed, slapped at his arm. "Well, he must be in hiding. I haven't seen anyone fitting that particular description around these parts."

Lucas let go of her, then turned to face her. "Maybe you need to get out more, find this man, bring him out of hiding. Maybe it's time for *you* to come out of hiding, too."

"Maybe," Lacey replied, her blue eyes bright with an unreadable light. Then she kissed her brother again. "Thank you, Lucas."

"For what?"

"For being you. I love you, you know."

Lucas nodded as they approached the rest of the group. "I do know. It took me a very long time to realize that I am loved, and it took me a long time to appreciate life, but now, ah, now…life is good."

Lorna heard his remarks and nodded, smiling at her husband. "I couldn't agree more."

Lacey shot her brother a wistful look.

Aunt Hilda smiled at the newlyweds. "My Lucas is happy at last. He's found some joie de vivre."

"Yes, indeed I have." Lucas winked at his sisters, then reached a hand toward Willa. "Let's get out of here."

His wife gave him a perplexed look, adjusted her cloche hat, then laughed. "Are you impatient, Mr. Dorsette?"

Lucas leaned close, inhaled the scent that made him think of secret gardens. "Why, yes, as a matter of fact, I am very impatient, Mrs. Dorsette. I want to take you away from all of this, to my lair in the swamp." He put his mouth close to her teardrop garnet earrings. "I want to ravish my new bride."

Willa's blue eyes lit up. She grinned. "What about our guests? What about that beautiful red velvet cake your sister so lovingly baked?"

"The guests are welcome to stay as long as they want, and the cake... Well, if I know Lorna, she's already sent the top layer to our little hideaway...along with some other delectable snacks for nibbling later." Then he kissed the nape of her neck. "But I have something else in mind for nibbling."

"You are so wicked."

"*Non, ma chèrie,* just madly in love with my wife."

"Can we go for a ride?" Willa asked, her gaze turning serious.

"In the plane?"

"Well, yes. That would be fun. But I was thinking of a ride on Zephyr, with Tulip barking and running behind us."

"Whatever the lady wants," Lucas said. Then to the amazement of his family and friends, he swept his bride up in his arms and proceeded to carry her down the garden path.

Toward forever.

* * * * *

Dear Reader,

I had the idea for this story a couple of years ago. I wanted to write about someone who'd survived breast cancer. Right in the middle of writing the book, a friend was diagnosed with breast cancer. Since I write a weekly column for the local paper, I did some research and found out that eight other women I knew were breast cancer survivors. I wrote about those brave women in my column during Breast Cancer Awareness Month (October). They were never far from my thoughts while I was writing this book.

In spite of the scary aspects of breast cancer, women should be aware that advancements in technology and medicine have made treatment of this disease much more viable and successful. Early detection is a factor in being able to have a complete recovery. But just like Willa in my story, many women think the worst and get scared and confused when they discover a lump in their breast.

So I urge each of you to do self-examinations and get those mammograms. There are many good books on the subject to help guide women through the proper procedures and decisions, and many doctors who are willing to give advice.

And there is always the best guidance—that which comes from a higher source of strength. Even in the worst of times, God will not leave us comfortless. Even in the worst of circumstances, if we are still and listening, He truly does give us something beautiful. He gives us life and love.

I hope the story of Willa and Lucas has given you hope that while our time here on earth is precious and precarious, we should hold fast to it and make something good out of it, no matter the number of days we have left. Go out today and find something beautiful to celebrate. Be a survivor.

Until next time, may the angels watch over you while you sleep.

Lenora Worth

Lucas's Favorite White Chocolate Bread Pudding

Small loaf of day-old French Bread
1 cup of heavy cream
1 cup of milk
4 eggs beaten
6 ounces premium white chocolate divided
1/2 cup sugar
1 teaspoon vanilla

Spray a 13" x 9" baking dish with cooking spray. Break bread into small pieces and place in baking dish. (Can toast bread to make it more crunchy if it's too fresh.)

Heat cream, milk and sugar until bubbly. Add 4 oz. of chocolate and stir until completely melted. (Save other 2 oz. for sauce.)

Slowly mix beaten eggs with milk mixture, until creamy. Add vanilla. Pour the milk and egg mixture over the bread in baking dish.

Let sit for 30 minutes.

Bake 350 degrees for about an hour, or until it begins to brown on top.

Sauce:
1/2 cup of cream or Half & Half
2 ounces white chocolate
Mix together until chocolate is completely melted.

Pour this over the cooked pudding, then take a knife and punch holes in pudding so sauce can soak through bread.

Can be served warm, or cold from the refrigerator!

If you enjoyed reading

SOMETHING BEAUTIFUL,

you'll love Lenora Worth's next book from her exciting In the Garden *series:*

LACEY'S RETREAT

*Brought to you by
Steeple Hill Love Inspired®…
Lacey Dorsette York is minding her own
business in a New Orleans church when
a dashing man in a tuxedo comes
running at her, clutching his shoulder
in pain. She takes Gavin Prescott under
her wing…and into her heart. But is
this handsome mystery man leading her
into dangerous territory…?*

Don't miss it!

*On sale September 2002
ISBN: 0-373-87191-0*

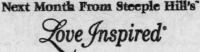